# JURASSIC PARK

### VOLUME 1

## DANGER

### ADAPTED BY
## WALTER SIMONSON,
## GIL KANE AND GEORGE PEREZ

Spotlight

IDW

**visit us at www.abdopublishing.com**

Reinforced library bound editions published in 2014 by Spotlight, a division of the ABDO Group, PO Box 398166, Minneapolis, Minnesota 55439. Published by agreement with IDW Publishing. www.idwpublishing.com



Printed in the United States of America, North Mankato, Minnesota.
052013
092013
This book contains at least 10% recycled materials.



**Library of Congress Cataloging-in-Publication Data**

Simonson, Walter.
Jurassic Park / adapted by Walter Simonson, Gil Kane, and George Perez.
pages cm
ISBN 978-1-61479-183-6 (vol. 1: Danger) -- ISBN 978-1-61479-184-3 (vol. 2: The miracle of cloning) -- ISBN 978-1-61479-185-0 (vol. 3: Don't move!) -- ISBN 978-1-61479-186-7 (vol. 4: Leaving Jurassic Park)
1. Graphic novels. I. Kane, Gil. II. Perez, George, 1954- III. Title.
PZ7.7.S5465Jur 2013
741.5'973--dc23

2013011263

All Spotlight books are reinforced library binding and manufactured in the United States of America.

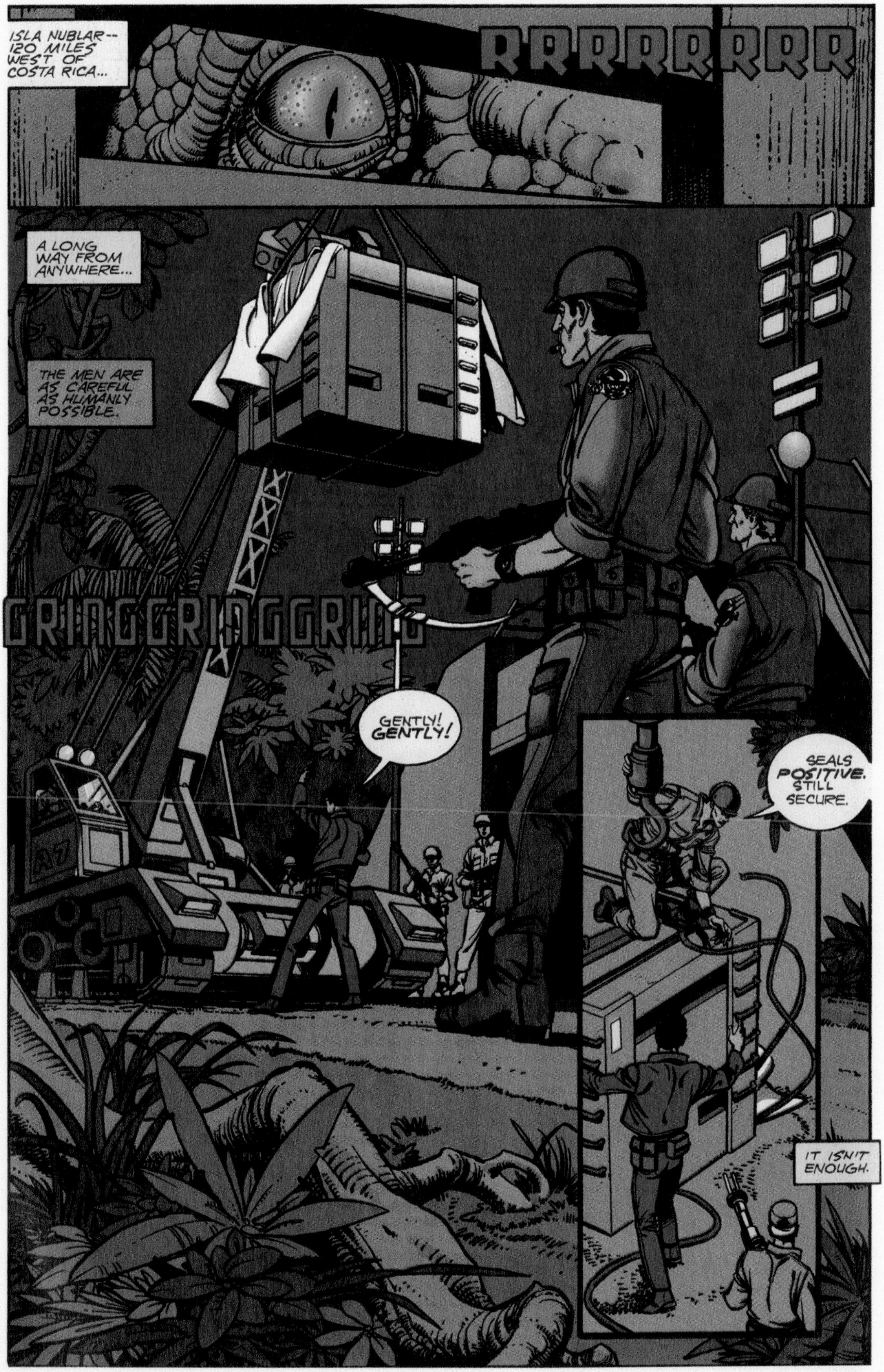

ISLA NUBLAR--
120 MILES
WEST OF
COSTA RICA...
RRRRRRRR
A LONG
WAY FROM
ANYWHERE...
THE MEN ARE
AS CAREFUL
AS HUMANLY
POSSIBLE.
GRINGGRINGGRING
GENTLY! GENTLY!
SEALS POSITIVE. STILL SECURE.
IT ISN'T ENOUGH.

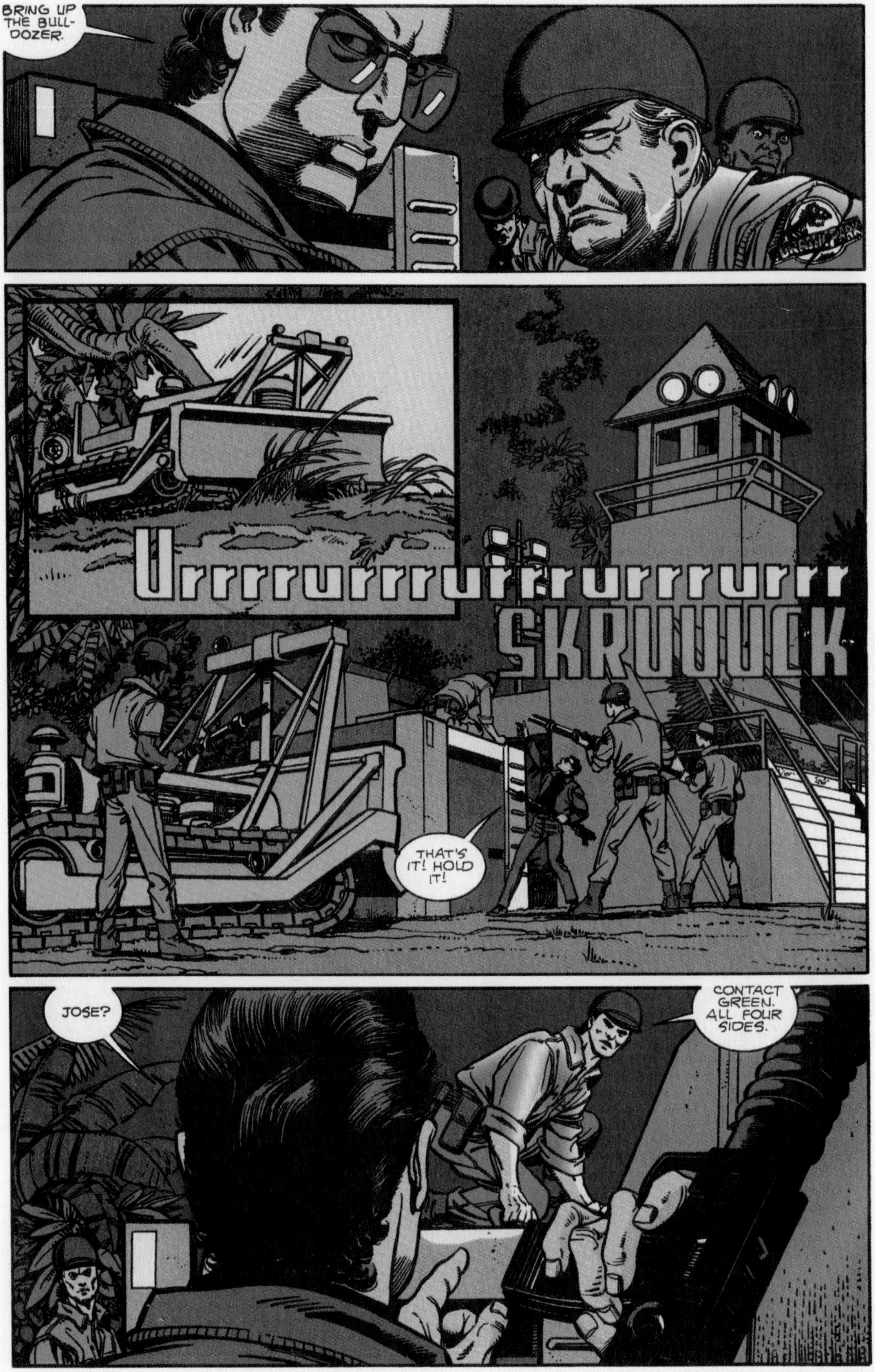
BRING UP THE BULL-DOZER.
Urrrrurrrrurrrrurrrr
SKRUUUCK
THAT'S IT! HOLD IT!
JOSE?
CONTACT GREEN. ALL FOUR SIDES.

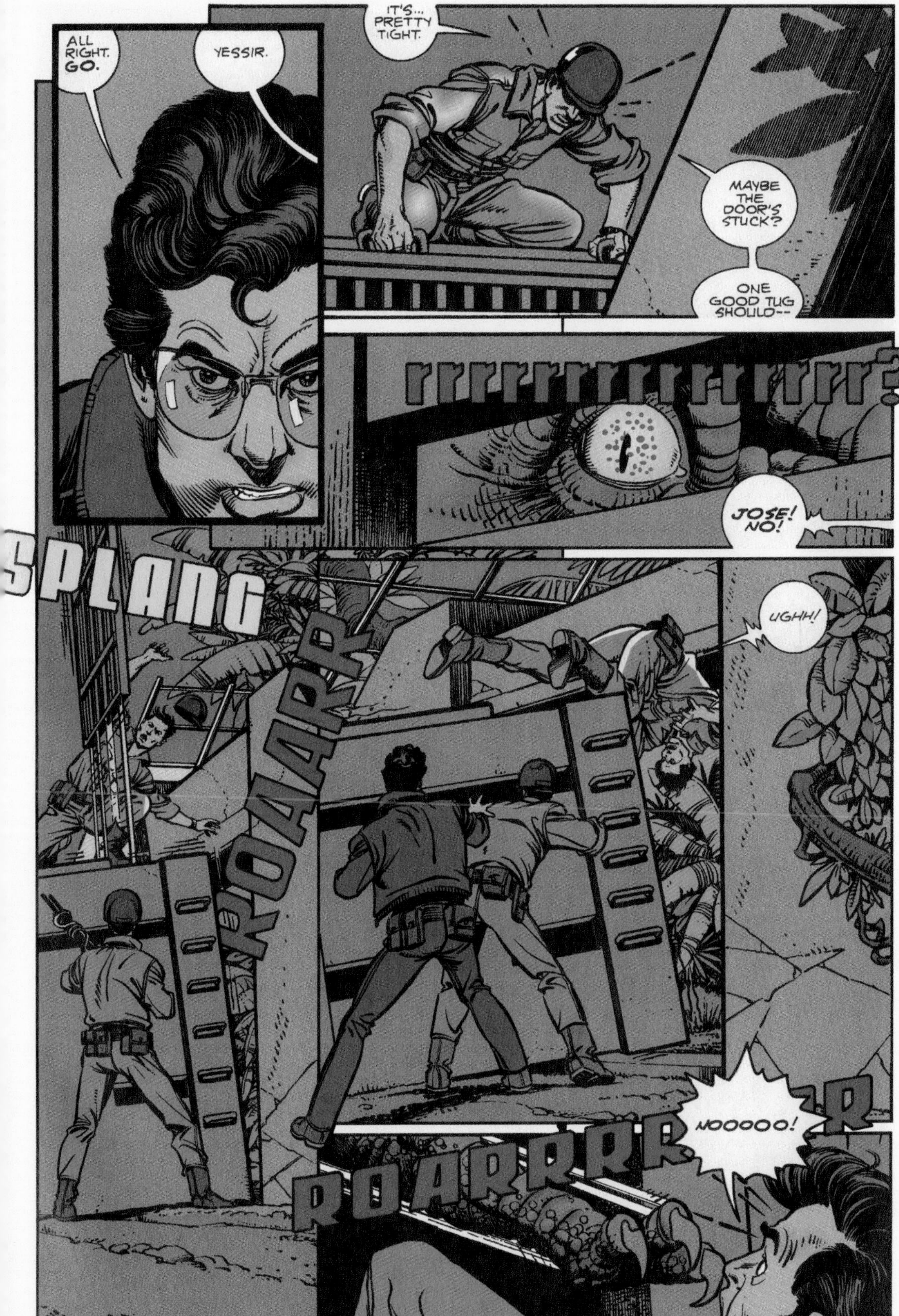
ALL RIGHT. GO.
YESSIR.
IT'S... PRETTY TIGHT.
MAYBE THE DOOR'S STUCK?
ONE GOOD TUG SHOULD--
rrrrrrrrrrrrrrr?
JOSE! NO!
SPLANG
ROAARR
UGHH!
NOOOOO!
ROARRRR

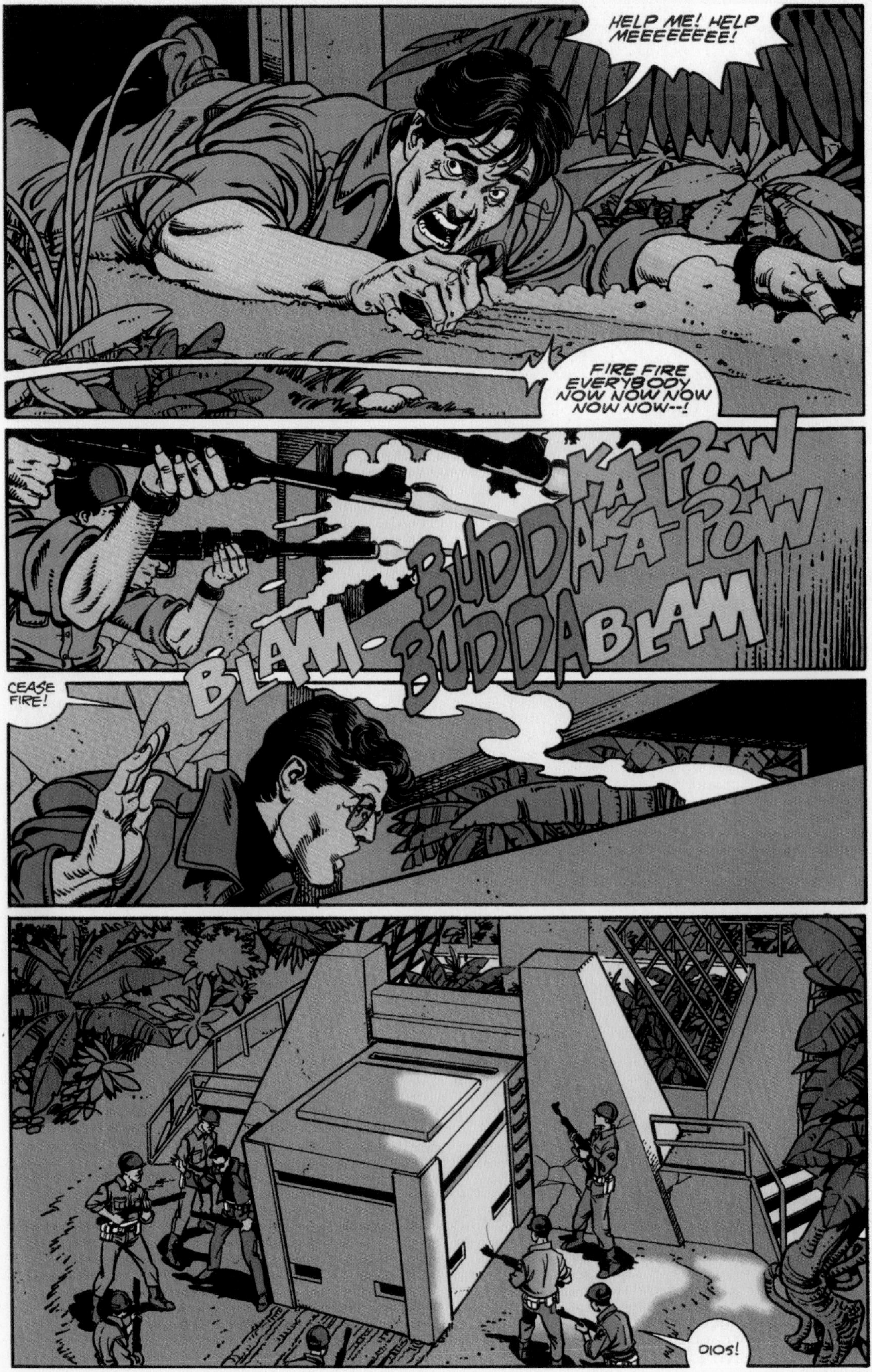
HELP ME! HELP MEEEEEEEE!
FIRE FIRE EVERYBODY NOW NOW NOW NOW NOW--!
KA-POW
BUDDAKA-POW
BLAM-
BUDDABLAM
CEASE FIRE!
DIOS!

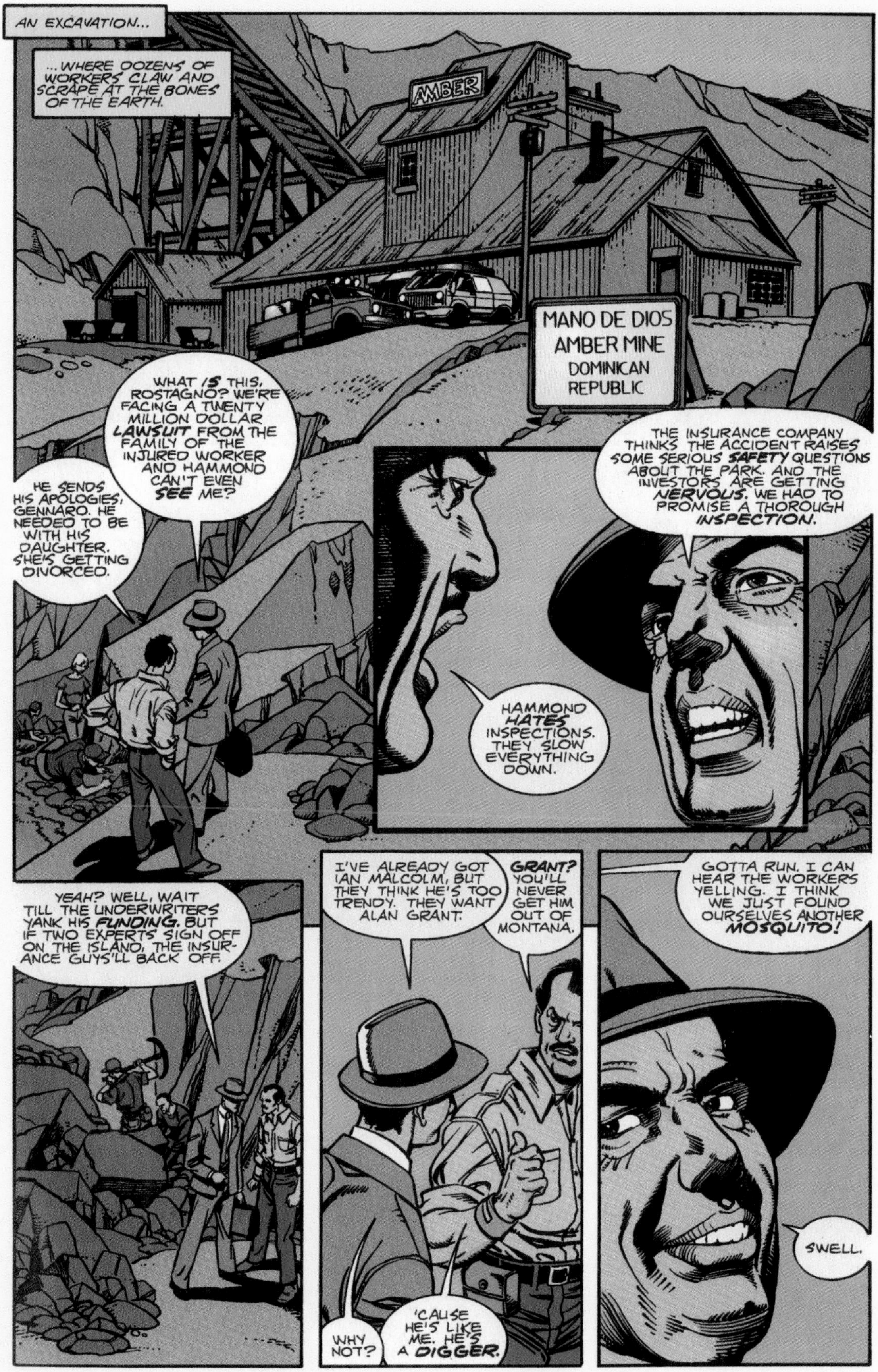
AN EXCAVATION...
...WHERE DOZENS OF WORKERS CLAW AND SCRAPE AT THE BONES OF THE EARTH.
AMBER
MANO DE DIOS AMBER MINE DOMINICAN REPUBLIC
WHAT IS THIS, ROSTAGNO? WE'RE FACING A TWENTY MILLION DOLLAR LAWSUIT FROM THE FAMILY OF THE INJURED WORKER AND HAMMOND CAN'T EVEN SEE ME?
HE SENDS HIS APOLOGIES, GENNARO. HE NEEDED TO BE WITH HIS DAUGHTER. SHE'S GETTING DIVORCED.
THE INSURANCE COMPANY THINKS THE ACCIDENT RAISES SOME SERIOUS SAFETY QUESTIONS ABOUT THE PARK. AND THE INVESTORS ARE GETTING NERVOUS. WE HAD TO PROMISE A THOROUGH INSPECTION.
HAMMOND HATES INSPECTIONS. THEY SLOW EVERYTHING DOWN.
YEAH? WELL, WAIT TILL THE UNDERWRITERS YANK HIS FUNDING. BUT IF TWO EXPERTS SIGN OFF ON THE ISLAND, THE INSURANCE GUYS'LL BACK OFF.
I'VE ALREADY GOT IAN MALCOLM, BUT THEY THINK HE'S TOO TRENDY. THEY WANT ALAN GRANT.
GRANT? YOU'LL NEVER GET HIM OUT OF MONTANA.
WHY NOT?
'CAUSE HE'S LIKE ME. HE'S A DIGGER.
GOTTA RUN. I CAN HEAR THE WORKERS YELLING. I THINK WE JUST FOUND OURSELVES ANOTHER MOSQUITO!
SWELL.

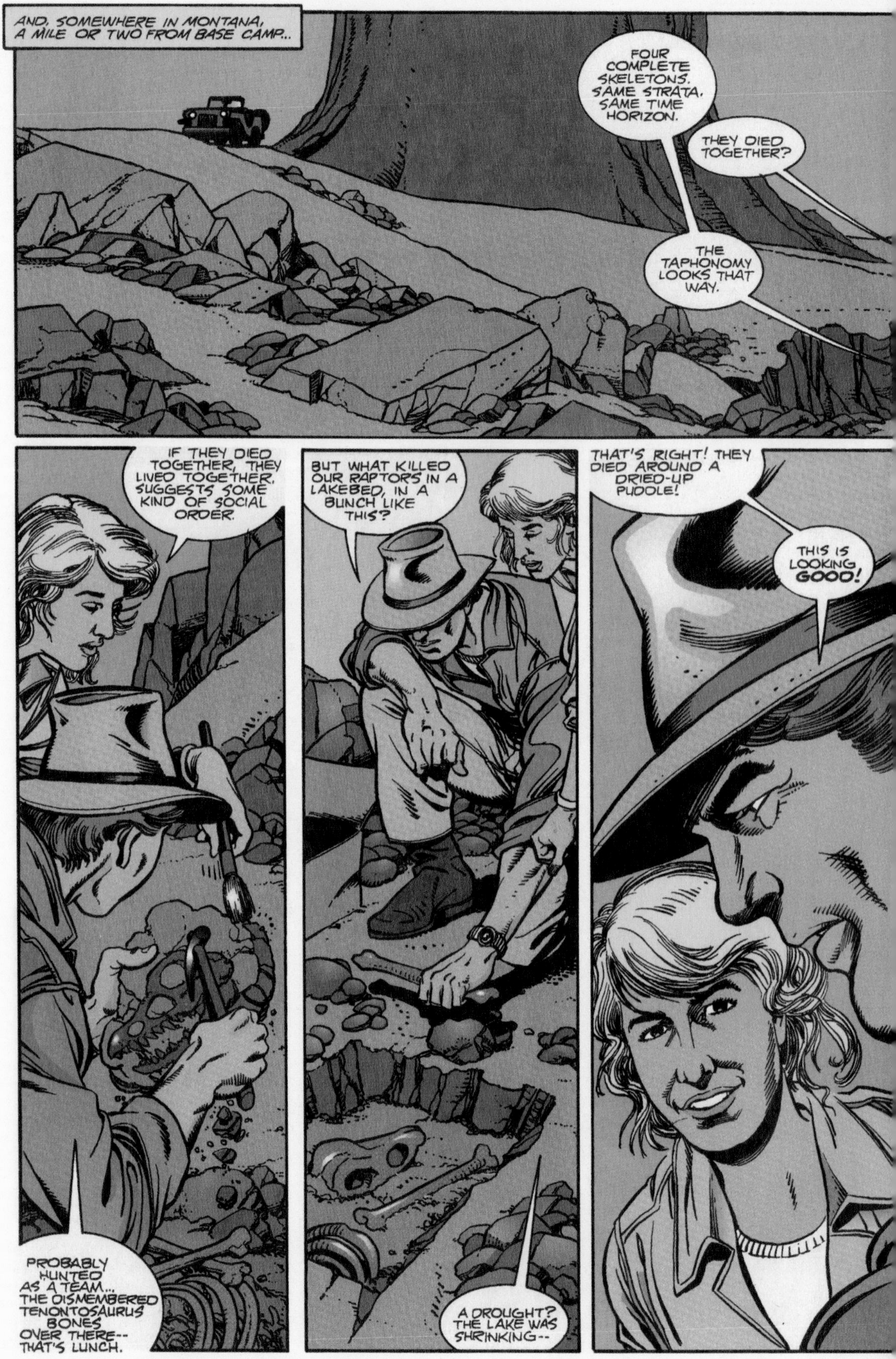
AND, SOMEWHERE IN MONTANA, A MILE OR TWO FROM BASE CAMP...
FOUR COMPLETE SKELETONS. SAME STRATA. SAME TIME HORIZON.
THEY DIED TOGETHER?
THE TAPHONOMY LOOKS THAT WAY.
IF THEY DIED TOGETHER, THEY LIVED TOGETHER. SUGGESTS SOME KIND OF SOCIAL ORDER.
PROBABLY HUNTED AS A TEAM... THE DISMEMBERED TENONTOSAURUS BONES OVER THERE-- THAT'S LUNCH.
BUT WHAT KILLED OUR RAPTORS IN A LAKEBED, IN A BUNCH LIKE THIS?
A DROUGHT? THE LAKE WAS SHRINKING--
THAT'S RIGHT! THEY DIED AROUND A DRIED-UP PUDDLE!
THIS IS LOOKING GOOD!

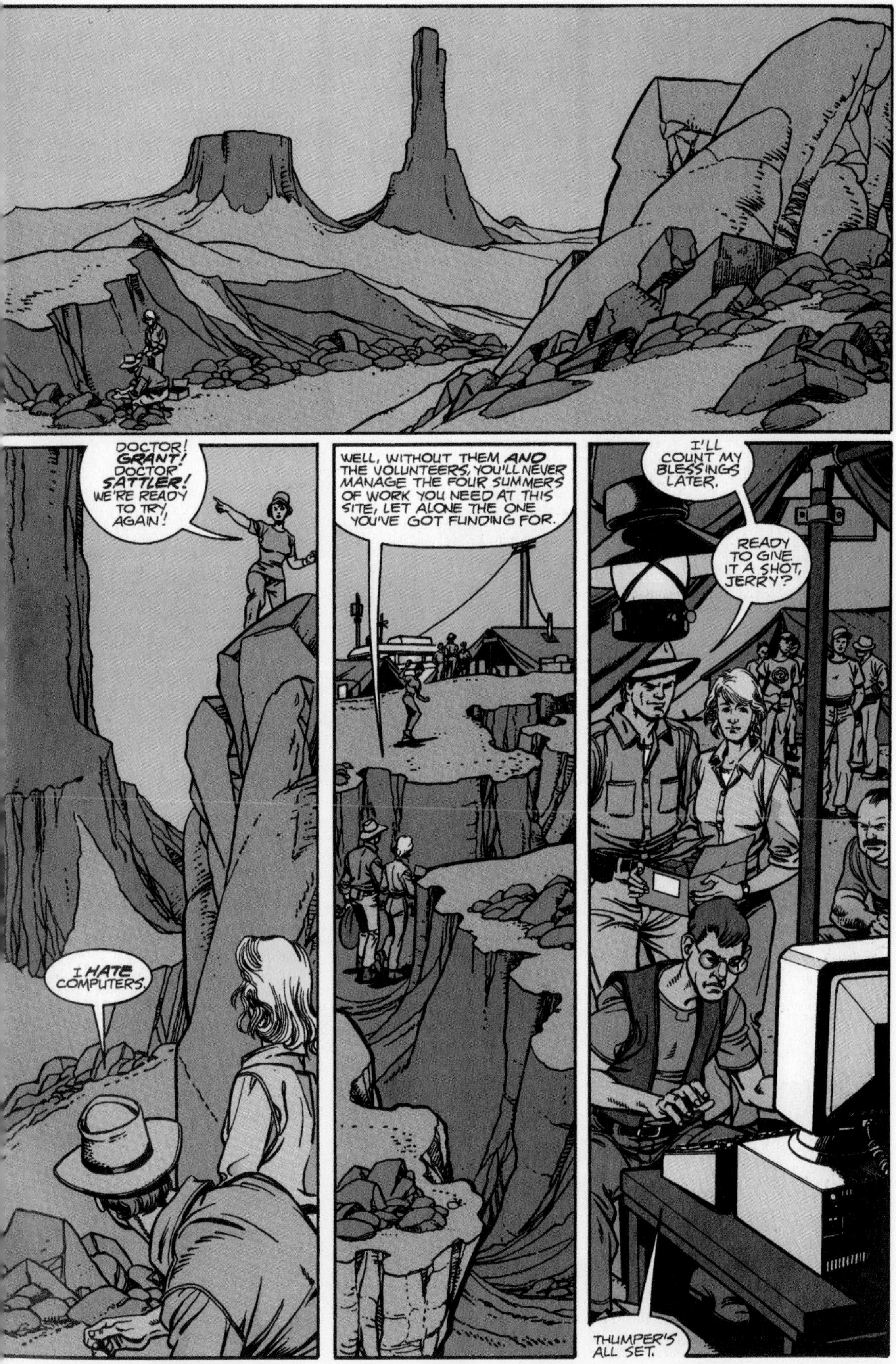
DOCTOR! GRANT! DOCTOR SATTLER! WE'RE READY TO TRY AGAIN!
I HATE COMPUTERS.
WELL, WITHOUT THEM AND THE VOLUNTEERS, YOU'LL NEVER MANAGE THE FOUR SUMMERS OF WORK YOU NEED AT THIS SITE, LET ALONE THE ONE YOU'VE GOT FUNDING FOR.
I'LL COUNT MY BLESSINGS LATER.
READY TO GIVE IT A SHOT, JERRY?
THUMPER'S ALL SET.

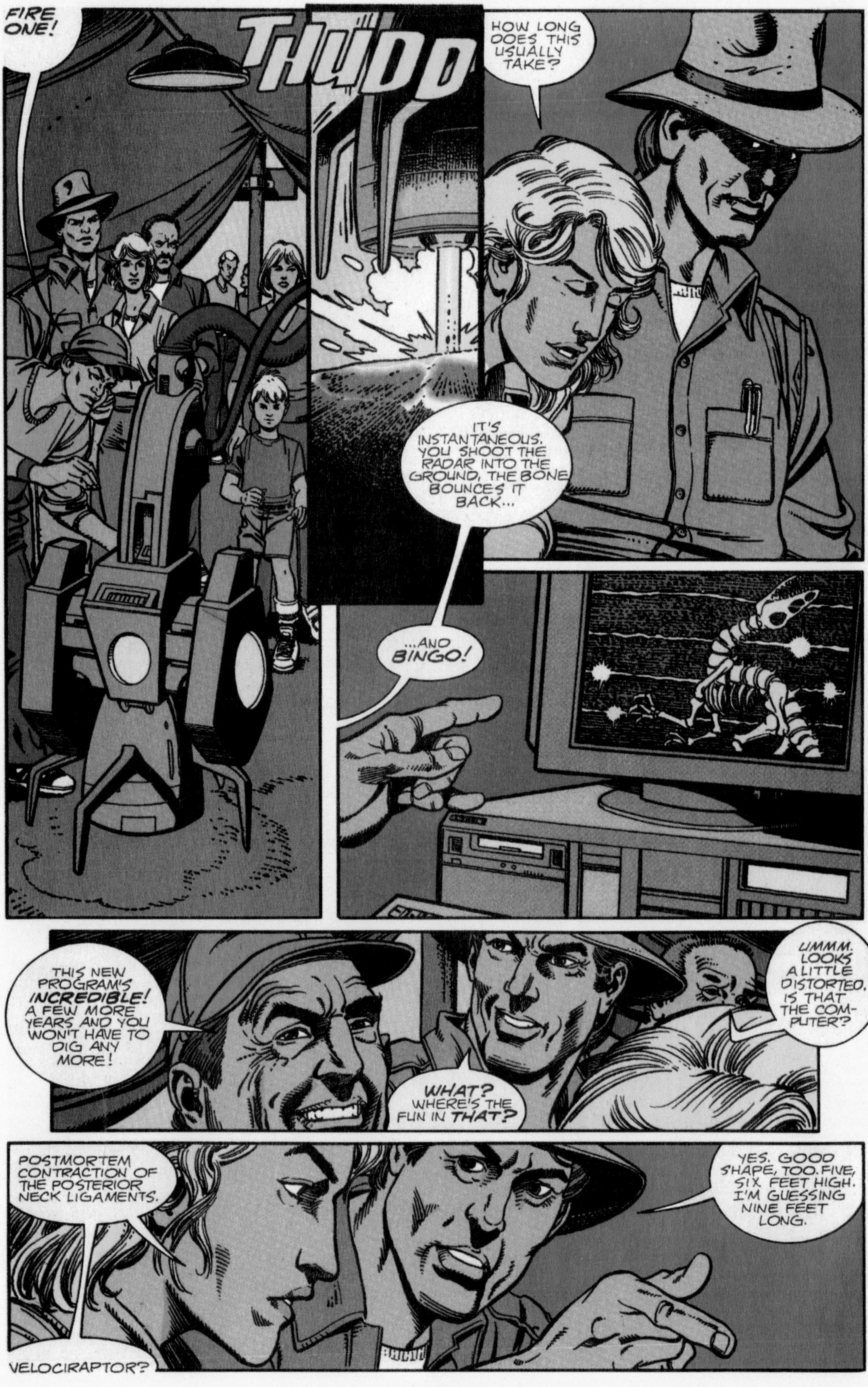
FIRE ONE!
THUDD
HOW LONG DOES THIS USUALLY TAKE?
IT'S INSTANTANEOUS. YOU SHOOT THE RADAR INTO THE GROUND, THE BONE BOUNCES IT BACK...
...AND BINGO!
THIS NEW PROGRAM'S INCREDIBLE! A FEW MORE YEARS AND YOU WON'T HAVE TO DIG ANY MORE!
WHAT? WHERE'S THE FUN IN THAT?
UMMM. LOOKS A LITTLE DISTORTED. IS THAT THE COM-PUTER?
POSTMORTEM CONTRACTION OF THE POSTERIOR NECK LIGAMENTS.
YES. GOOD SHAPE, TOO. FIVE, SIX FEET HIGH. I'M GUESSING NINE FEET LONG.
VELOCIRAPTOR?

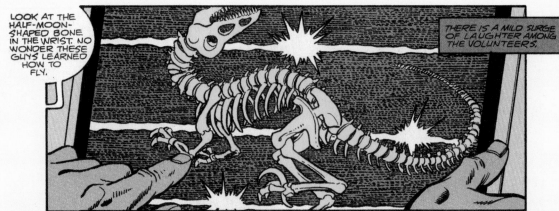

LOOK AT THE HALF-MOON-SHAPED BONE IN THE WRIST. NO WONDER THESE GUYS LEARNED HOW TO FLY.

THERE IS A MILD SURGE OF LAUGHTER AMONG THE VOLUNTEERS.

NOW, SERIOUSLY. SHOW OF HANDS. HOW MANY OF YOU HAVE READ MY BOOK?

COUGH COUGH

AHHH-HEMM

SIGH. DINOSAURS MAY HAVE MORE IN COMMON WITH PRESENT-DAY BIRDS THAN *REPTILES.* LOOK AT THE PUBIC BONE. TURNED BACKWARDS.

THE VERTEBRAE --FULL OF HOLLOWS AND AIR SACS. JUST LIKE *BIRDS.* EVEN THE WORD *"RAPTOR"* MEANS *"BIRD OF PREY."*

AH, THAT DOESN'T LOOK VERY *SCARY.* MORE LIKE A BIG *TURKEY!*

WELLLL, TRY TO IMAGINE YOURSELF IN THE JURASSIC PERIOD.

GRANT!

YOU'D KEEP STILL BECAUSE YOU THINK MAYBE HIS VISUAL ACUITY IS BASED ON *MOVEMENT,* LIKE A T-REX...

NO, REALLY. YOU'D GET YOUR FIRST LOOK AT THAT BIG TURKEY AS YOU MOVE INTO A CLEARING.

BUT THE *RAPTOR, HE* KNEW YOU WERE THERE A LONG TIME AGO.

...AND HE'LL *LOSE* YOU IF YOU DON'T MOVE.

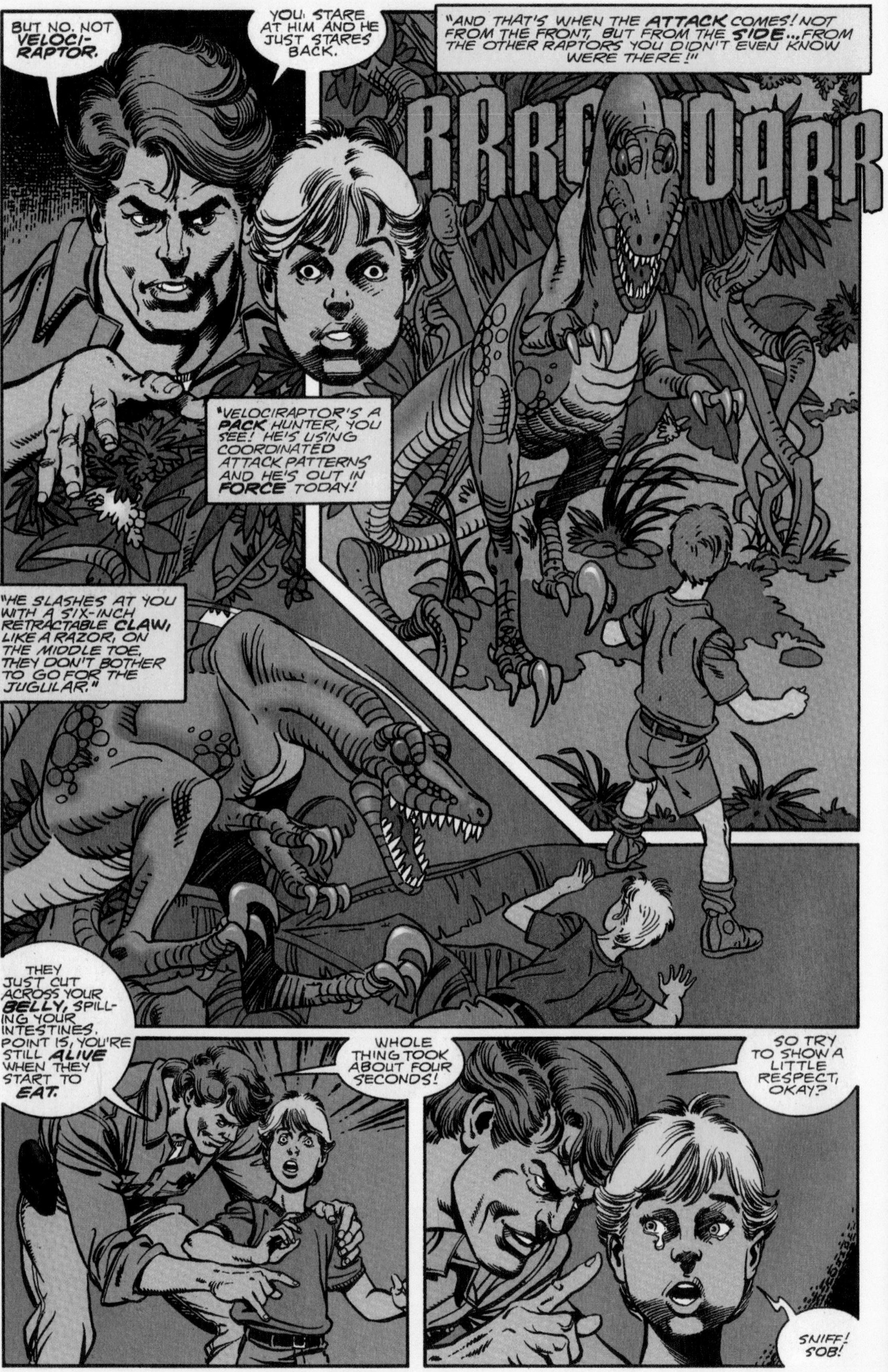
BUT NO. NOT VELOCI-RAPTOR.
YOU STARE AT HIM AND HE JUST STARES BACK.
"AND THAT'S WHEN THE ATTACK COMES! NOT FROM THE FRONT, BUT FROM THE SIDE...FROM THE OTHER RAPTORS YOU DIDN'T EVEN KNOW WERE THERE!!"
RRRROOARR
"VELOCIRAPTOR'S A PACK HUNTER, YOU SEE! HE'S USING COORDINATED ATTACK PATTERNS AND HE'S OUT IN FORCE TODAY!
"HE SLASHES AT YOU WITH A SIX-INCH RETRACTABLE CLAW, LIKE A RAZOR, ON THE MIDDLE TOE. THEY DON'T BOTHER TO GO FOR THE JUGULAR."
THEY JUST CUT ACROSS YOUR BELLY, SPILLING YOUR INTESTINES. POINT IS, YOU'RE STILL ALIVE WHEN THEY START TO EAT.
WHOLE THING TOOK ABOUT FOUR SECONDS!
SO TRY TO SHOW A LITTLE RESPECT, OKAY?
SNIFF! SOB!

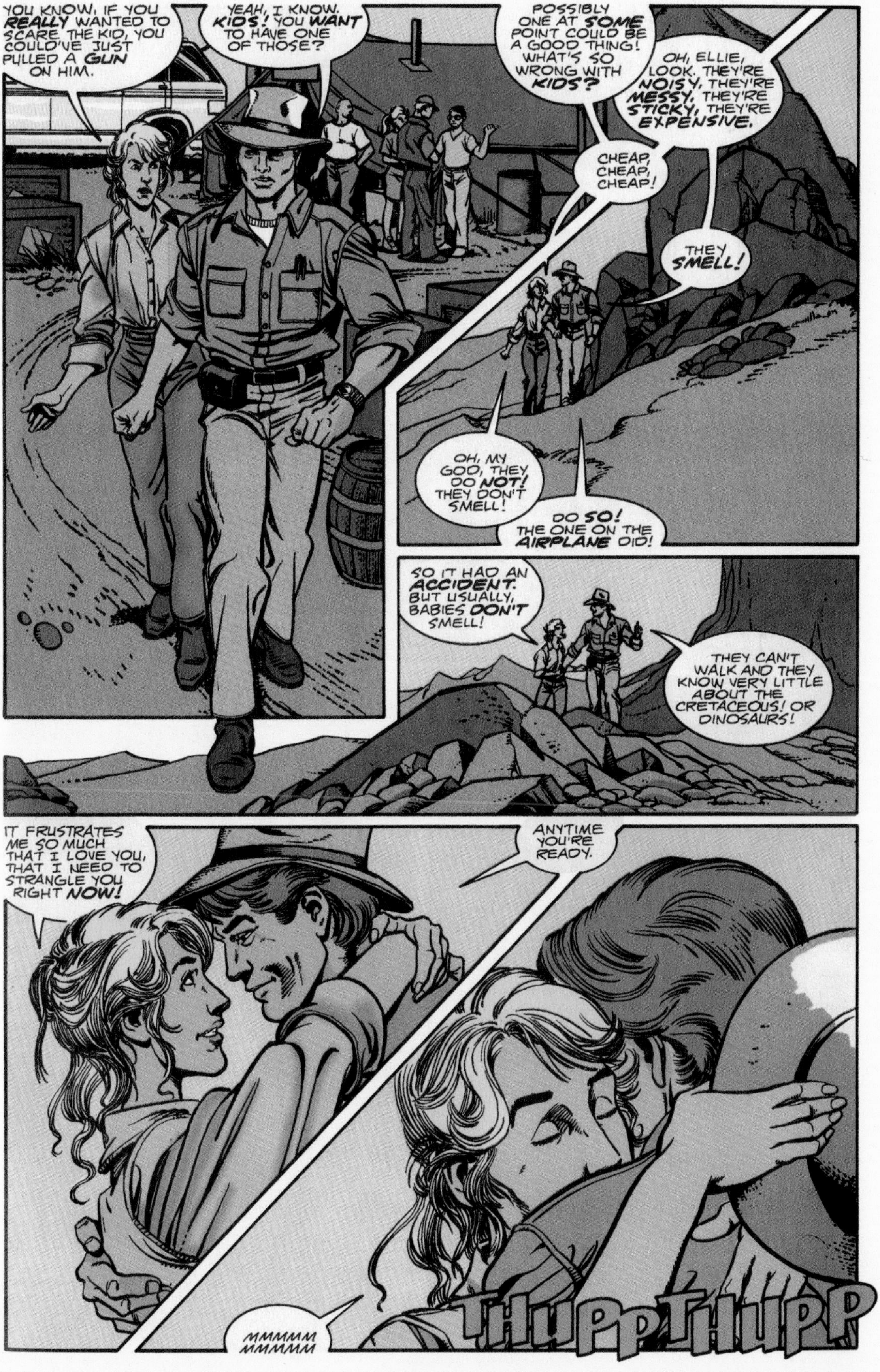
YOU KNOW, IF YOU REALLY WANTED TO SCARE THE KID, YOU COULD'VE JUST PULLED A GUN ON HIM.
YEAH, I KNOW. KIDS! YOU WANT TO HAVE ONE OF THOSE?
POSSIBLY ONE AT SOME POINT COULD BE A GOOD THING! WHAT'S SO WRONG WITH KIDS?
OH, ELLIE, LOOK. THEY'RE NOISY, THEY'RE MESSY, THEY'RE STICKY, THEY'RE EXPENSIVE.
CHEAP, CHEAP, CHEAP!
THEY SMELL!
OH, MY GOD, THEY DO NOT! THEY DON'T SMELL!
DO SO! THE ONE ON THE AIRPLANE DID!
SO IT HAD AN ACCIDENT. BUT USUALLY, BABIES DON'T SMELL!
THEY CAN'T WALK AND THEY KNOW VERY LITTLE ABOUT THE CRETACEOUS! OR DINOSAURS!
IT FRUSTRATES ME SO MUCH THAT I LOVE YOU, THAT I NEED TO STRANGLE YOU RIGHT NOW!
ANYTIME YOU'RE READY.
MMMMM MMMMM
THUPP THUPP

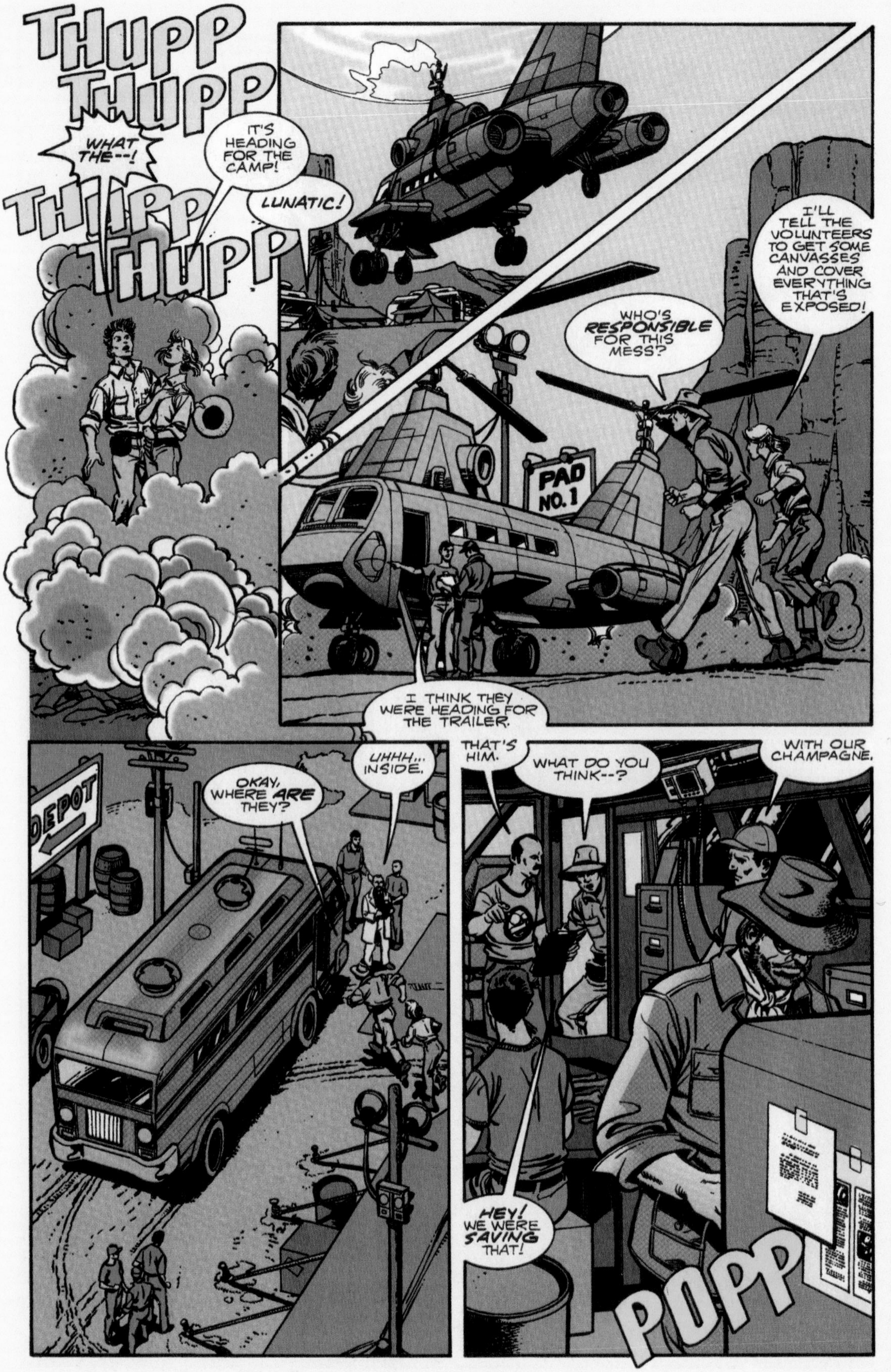
THUPP THUPP
WHAT THE--!
IT'S HEADING FOR THE CAMP!
LUNATIC!
THUPP THUPP
WHO'S RESPONSIBLE FOR THIS MESS?
I'LL TELL THE VOLUNTEERS TO GET SOME CANVASSES AND COVER EVERYTHING THAT'S EXPOSED!
PAD NO. 1
I THINK THEY WERE HEADING FOR THE TRAILER.
DEPOT
OKAY, WHERE ARE THEY?
UHHH... INSIDE.
THAT'S HIM.
WHAT DO YOU THINK--?
WITH OUR CHAMPAGNE.
HEY! WE WERE SAVING THAT!
POPP

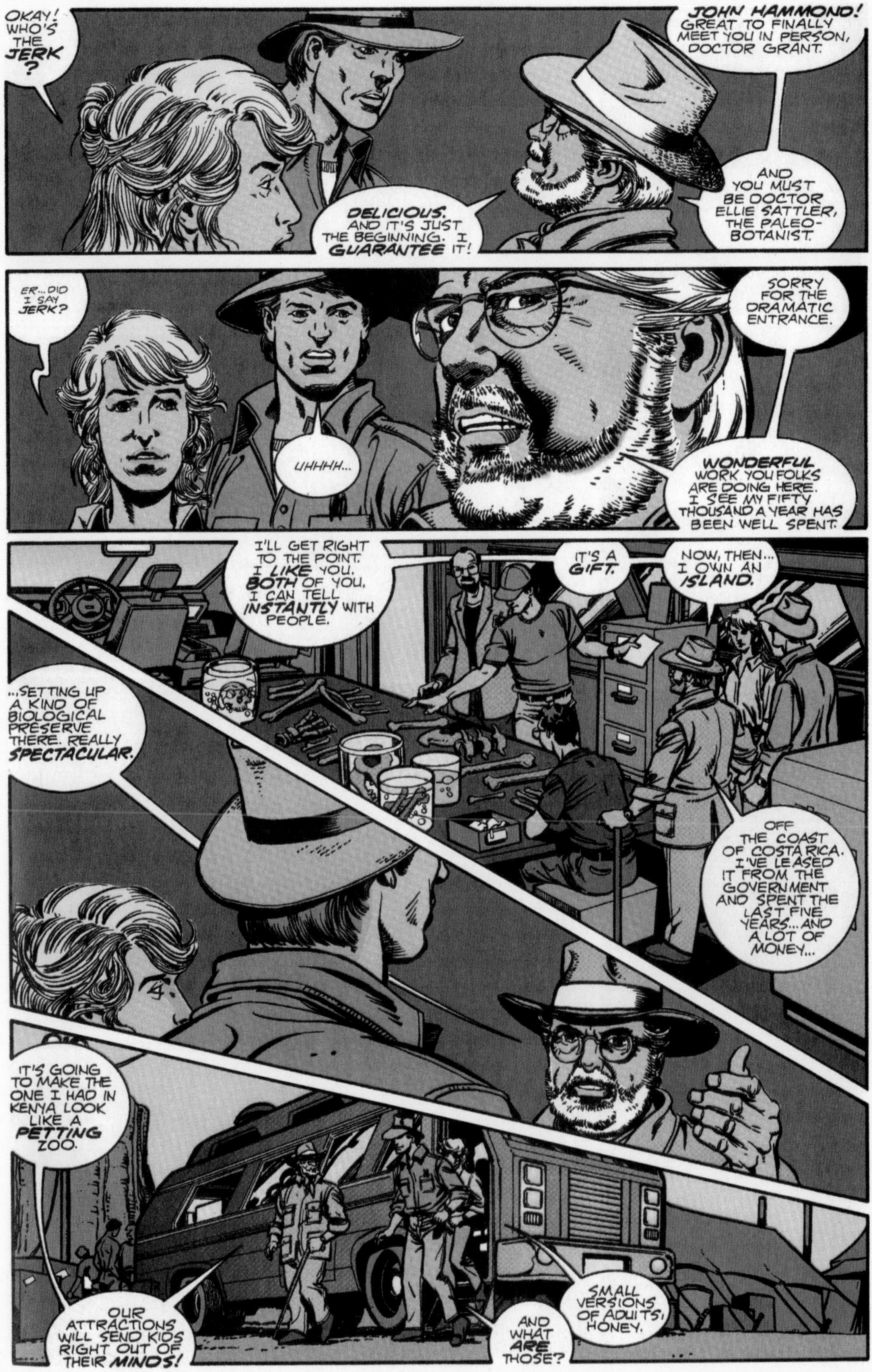

OKAY! WHO'S THE JERK?
JOHN HAMMOND! GREAT TO FINALLY MEET YOU IN PERSON, DOCTOR GRANT.
AND YOU MUST BE DOCTOR ELLIE SATTLER, THE PALEO-BOTANIST.
DELICIOUS. AND IT'S JUST THE BEGINNING. I GUARANTEE IT!
ER... DID I SAY JERK?
SORRY FOR THE DRAMATIC ENTRANCE.
UHHHH...
WONDERFUL WORK YOU FOLKS ARE DOING HERE. I SEE MY FIFTY THOUSAND A YEAR HAS BEEN WELL SPENT.
I'LL GET RIGHT TO THE POINT. I LIKE YOU. BOTH OF YOU. I CAN TELL INSTANTLY WITH PEOPLE.
IT'S A GIFT.
NOW, THEN... I OWN AN ISLAND.
OFF THE COAST OF COSTA RICA. I'VE LEASED IT FROM THE GOVERNMENT AND SPENT THE LAST FIVE YEARS... AND A LOT OF MONEY...
...SETTING UP A KIND OF BIOLOGICAL PRESERVE THERE. REALLY SPECTACULAR.
IT'S GOING TO MAKE THE ONE I HAD IN KENYA LOOK LIKE A PETTING ZOO.
OUR ATTRACTIONS WILL SEND KIDS RIGHT OUT OF THEIR MINDS!
AND WHAT ARE THOSE?
SMALL VERSIONS OF ADULTS, HONEY.

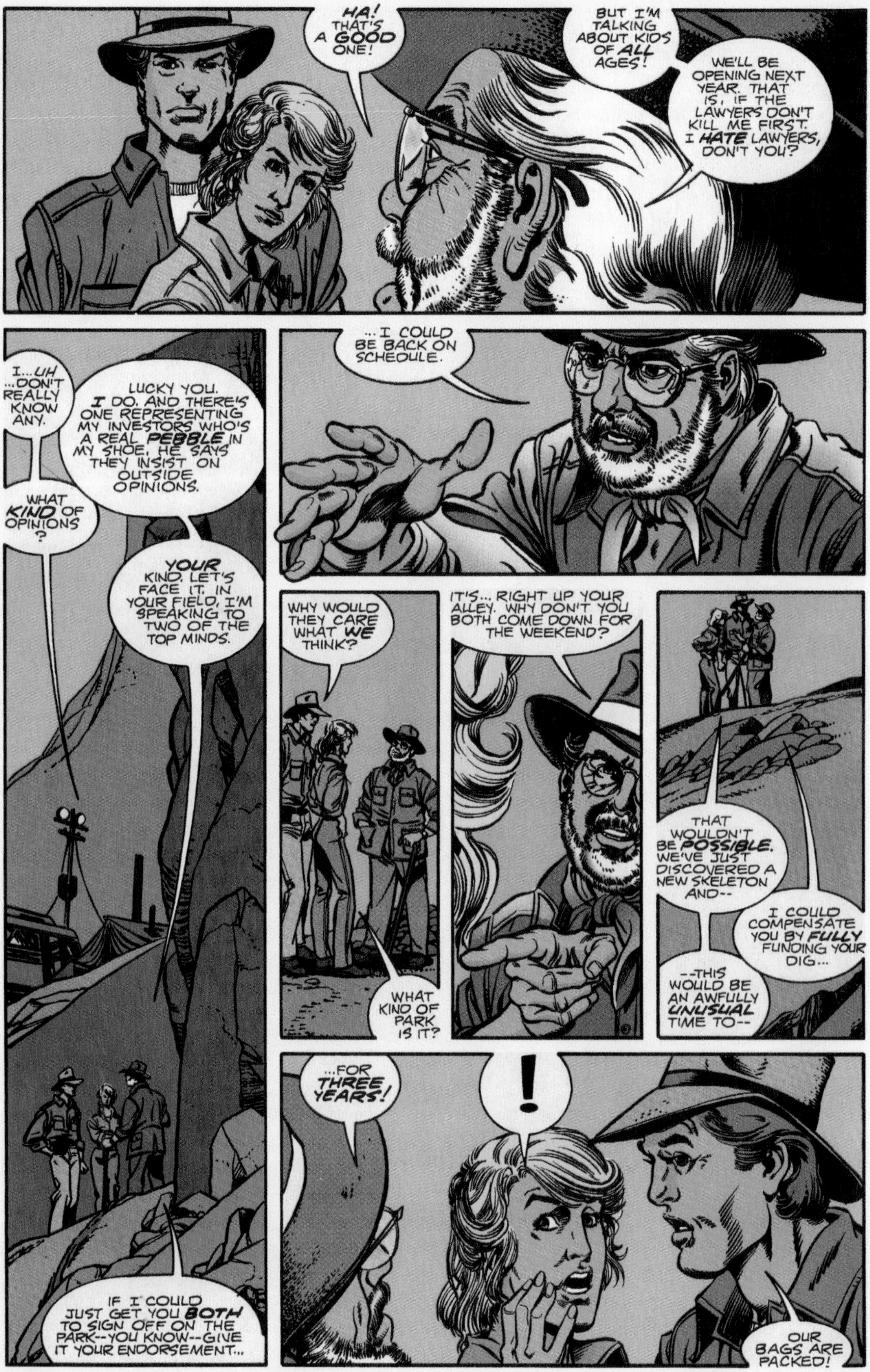
HA! THAT'S A GOOD ONE!
BUT I'M TALKING ABOUT KIDS OF ALL AGES!
WE'LL BE OPENING NEXT YEAR. THAT IS, IF THE LAWYERS DON'T KILL ME FIRST. I HATE LAWYERS, DON'T YOU?
I...UH ...DON'T REALLY KNOW ANY.
LUCKY YOU. I DO. AND THERE'S ONE REPRESENTING MY INVESTORS WHO'S A REAL PEBBLE IN MY SHOE. HE SAYS THEY INSIST ON OUTSIDE OPINIONS.
WHAT KIND OF OPINIONS ?
YOUR KIND. LET'S FACE IT. IN YOUR FIELD, I'M SPEAKING TO TWO OF THE TOP MINDS.
IF I COULD JUST GET YOU BOTH TO SIGN OFF ON THE PARK--YOU KNOW--GIVE IT YOUR ENDORSEMENT...
...I COULD BE BACK ON SCHEDULE.
WHY WOULD THEY CARE WHAT WE THINK?
WHAT KIND OF PARK IS IT?
IT'S... RIGHT UP YOUR ALLEY. WHY DON'T YOU BOTH COME DOWN FOR THE WEEKEND?
THAT WOULDN'T BE POSSIBLE. WE'VE JUST DISCOVERED A NEW SKELETON AND--
--THIS WOULD BE AN AWFULLY UNUSUAL TIME TO--
I COULD COMPENSATE YOU BY FULLY FUNDING YOUR DIG...
...FOR THREE YEARS!
!
OUR BAGS ARE PACKED!

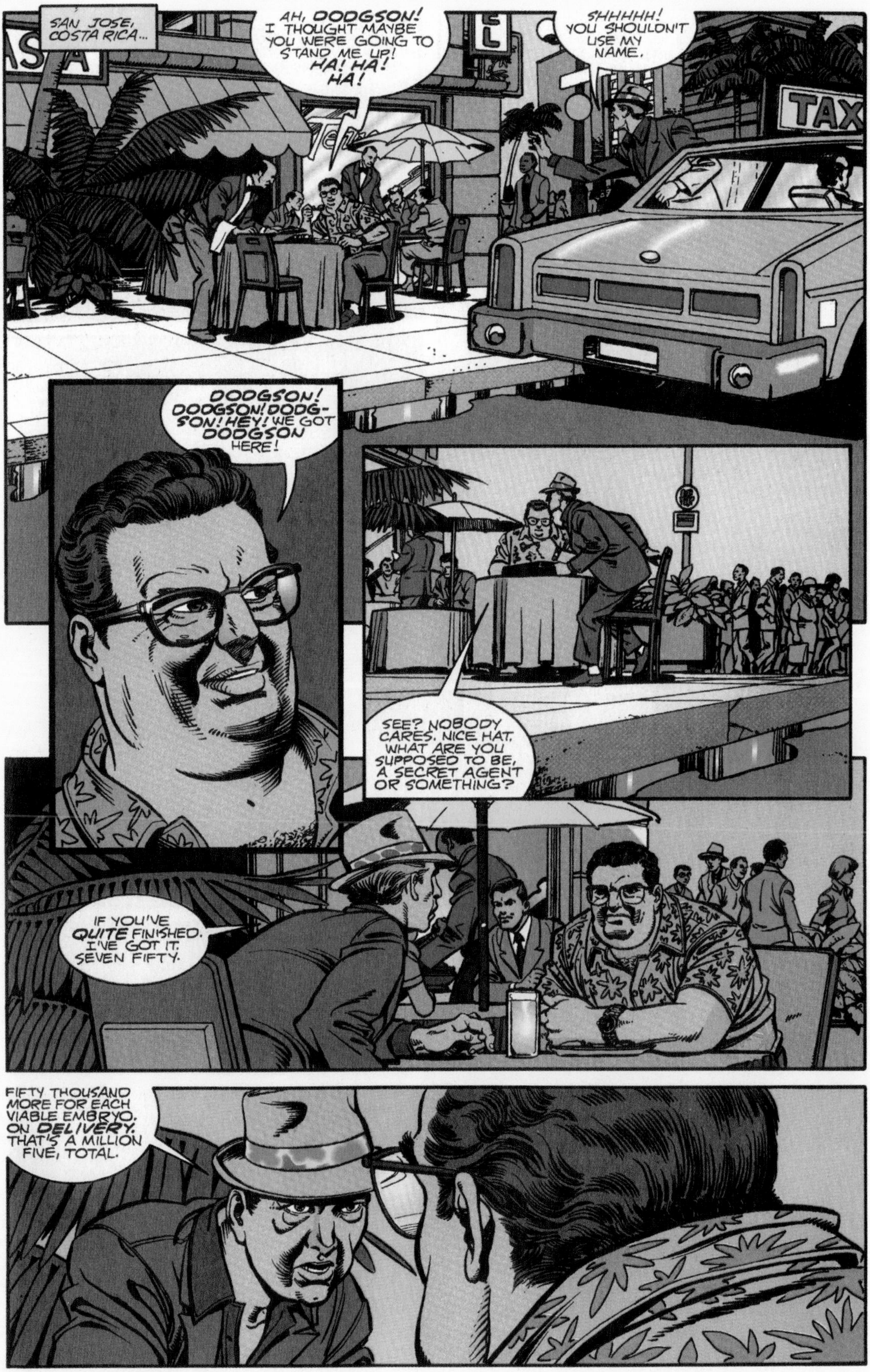
SAN JOSE, COSTA RICA...
AH, DODGSON! I THOUGHT MAYBE YOU WERE GOING TO STAND ME UP! HA! HA! HA!
SHHHHH! YOU SHOULDN'T USE MY NAME.
TAXI
DODGSON! DODGSON! DODGSON! HEY! WE GOT DODGSON HERE!
SEE? NOBODY CARES. NICE HAT. WHAT ARE YOU SUPPOSED TO BE, A SECRET AGENT OR SOMETHING?
IF YOU'VE QUITE FINISHED. I'VE GOT IT. SEVEN FIFTY.
FIFTY THOUSAND MORE FOR EACH VIABLE EMBRYO. ON DELIVERY. THAT'S A MILLION FIVE, TOTAL.

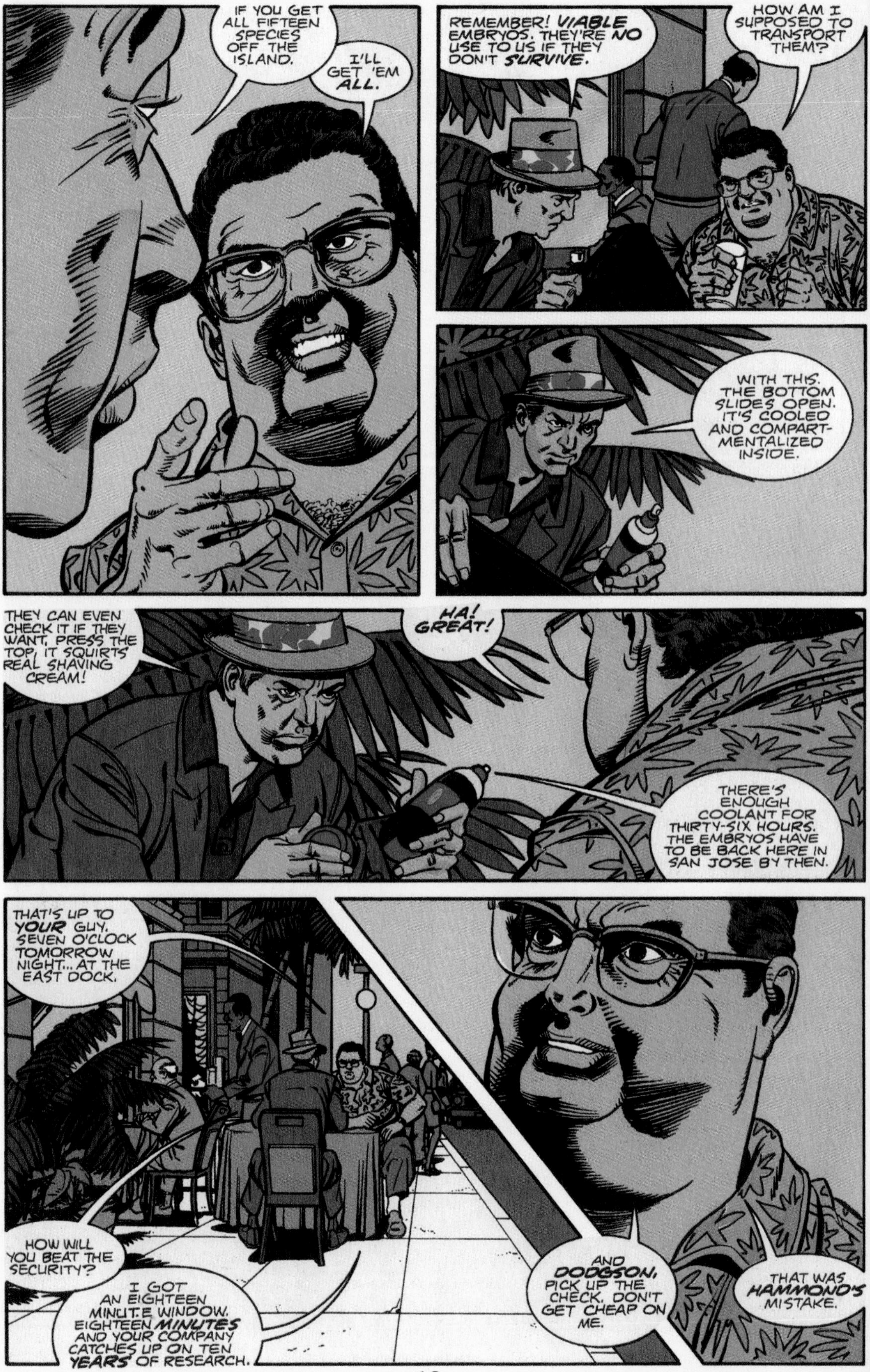
IF YOU GET ALL FIFTEEN SPECIES OFF THE ISLAND.
I'LL GET 'EM ALL.
REMEMBER! VIABLE EMBRYOS. THEY'RE NO USE TO US IF THEY DON'T SURVIVE.
HOW AM I SUPPOSED TO TRANSPORT THEM?
WITH THIS. THE BOTTOM SLIDES OPEN. IT'S COOLED AND COMPART-MENTALIZED INSIDE.
THEY CAN EVEN CHECK IT IF THEY WANT, PRESS THE TOP, IT SQUIRTS REAL SHAVING CREAM!
HA! GREAT!
THERE'S ENOUGH COOLANT FOR THIRTY-SIX HOURS. THE EMBRYOS HAVE TO BE BACK HERE IN SAN JOSE BY THEN.
THAT'S UP TO YOUR GUY. SEVEN O'CLOCK TOMORROW NIGHT... AT THE EAST DOCK.
HOW WILL YOU BEAT THE SECURITY?
I GOT AN EIGHTEEN MINUTE WINDOW. EIGHTEEN MINUTES AND YOUR COMPANY CATCHES UP ON TEN YEARS OF RESEARCH.
AND DODGSON, PICK UP THE CHECK. DON'T GET CHEAP ON ME.
THAT WAS HAMMOND'S MISTAKE.

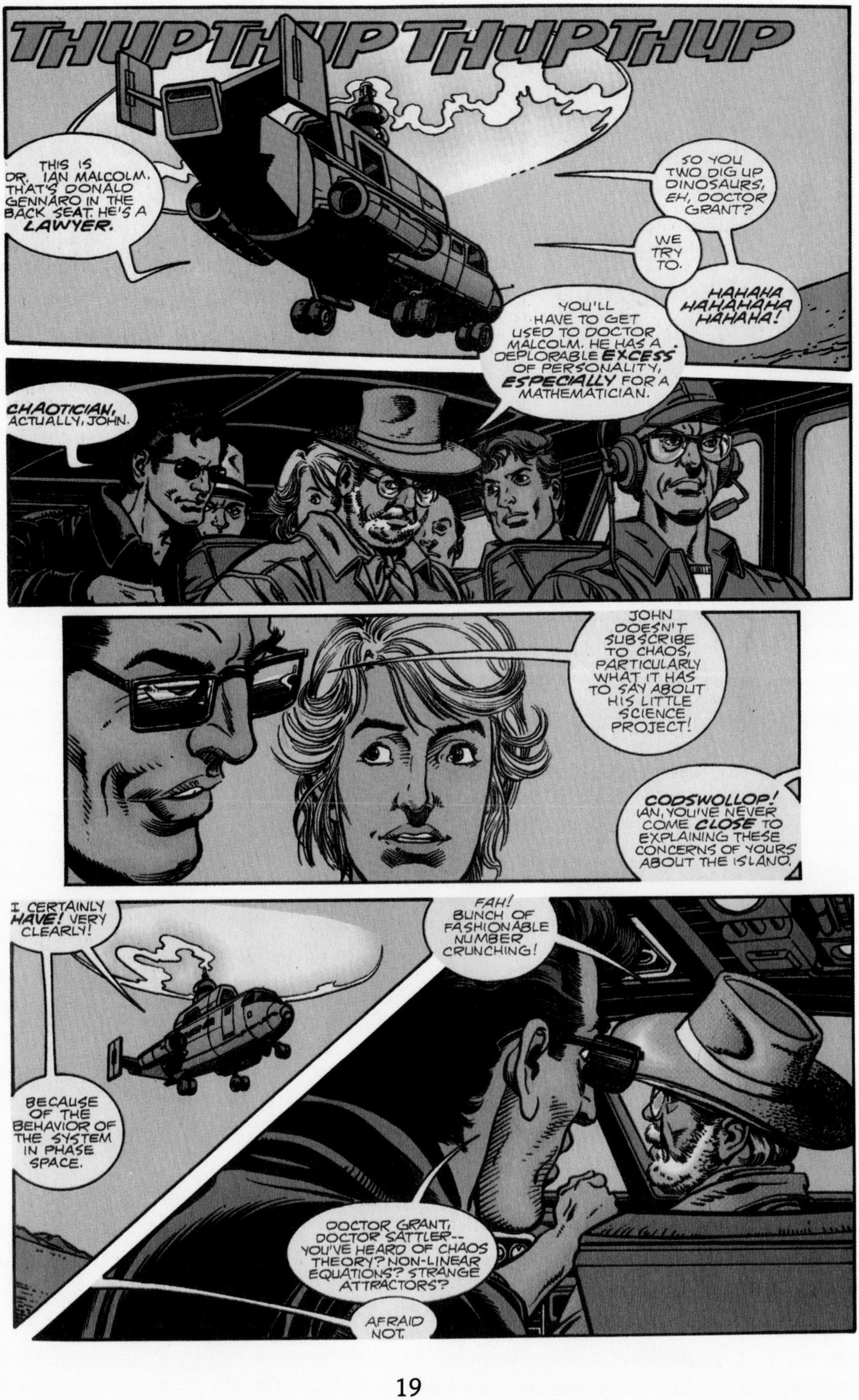
THUPTHUPTHUPTHUP
THIS IS DR. IAN MALCOLM. THAT'S DONALD GENNARO IN THE BACK SEAT. HE'S A LAWYER.
SO YOU TWO DIG UP DINOSAURS, EH, DOCTOR GRANT?
WE TRY TO.
HAHAHA HAHAHAHA HAHAHA!
YOU'LL HAVE TO GET USED TO DOCTOR MALCOLM. HE HAS A DEPLORABLE EXCESS OF PERSONALITY, ESPECIALLY FOR A MATHEMATICIAN.
CHAOTICIAN, ACTUALLY, JOHN.
JOHN DOESN'T SUBSCRIBE TO CHAOS, PARTICULARLY WHAT IT HAS TO SAY ABOUT HIS LITTLE SCIENCE PROJECT!
CODSWOLLOP! IAN, YOU'VE NEVER COME CLOSE TO EXPLAINING THESE CONCERNS OF YOURS ABOUT THE ISLAND.
I CERTAINLY HAVE! VERY CLEARLY!
FAH! BUNCH OF FASHIONABLE NUMBER CRUNCHING!
BECAUSE OF THE BEHAVIOR OF THE SYSTEM IN PHASE SPACE.
DOCTOR GRANT, DOCTOR SATTLER-- YOU'VE HEARD OF CHAOS THEORY? NON-LINEAR EQUATIONS? STRANGE ATTRACTORS?
AFRAID NOT.

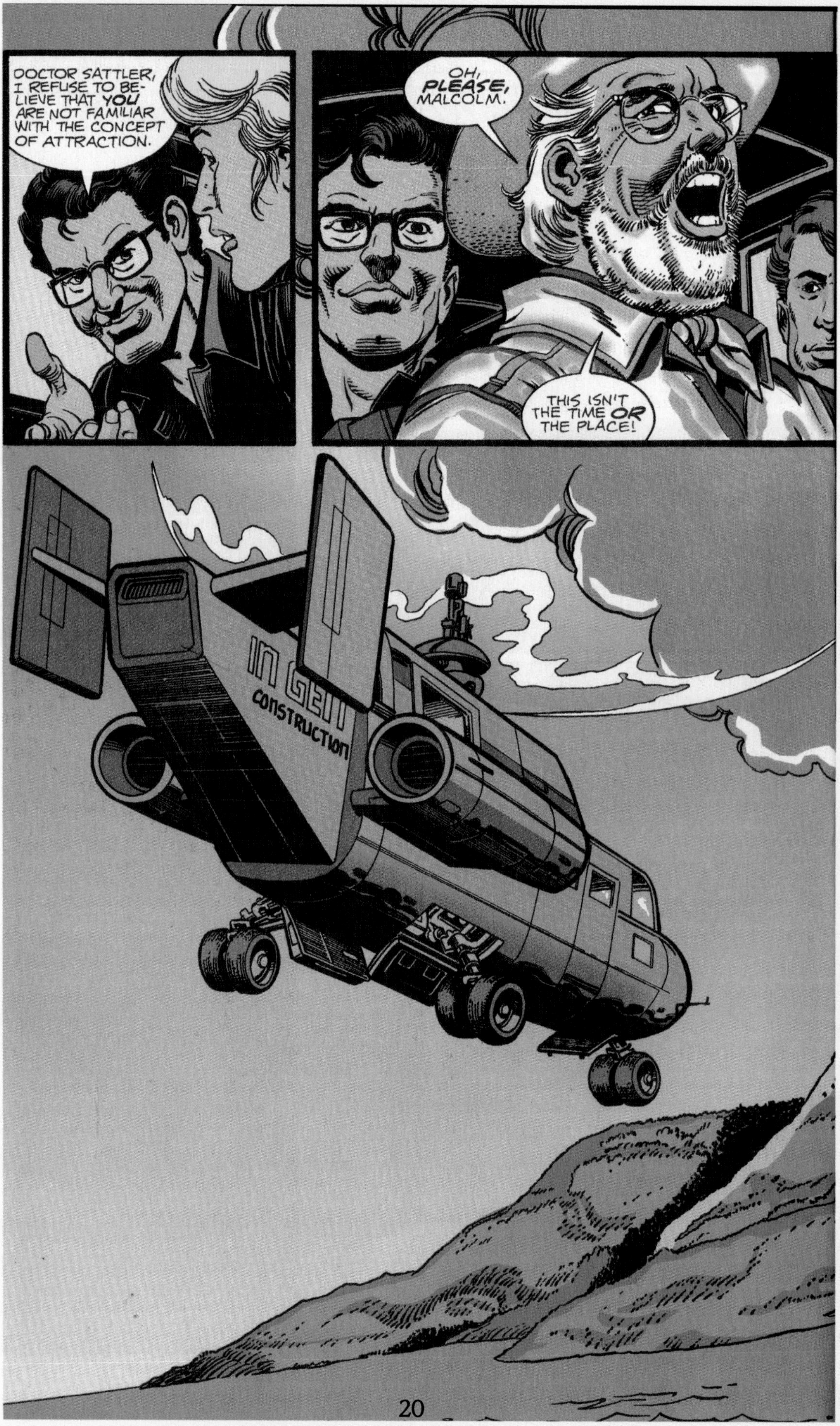
DOCTOR SATTLER, I REFUSE TO BE-LIEVE THAT YOU ARE NOT FAMILIAR WITH THE CONCEPT OF ATTRACTION.
OH, PLEASE, MALCOLM.
THIS ISN'T THE TIME OR THE PLACE!
IN GEN
CONSTRUCTION

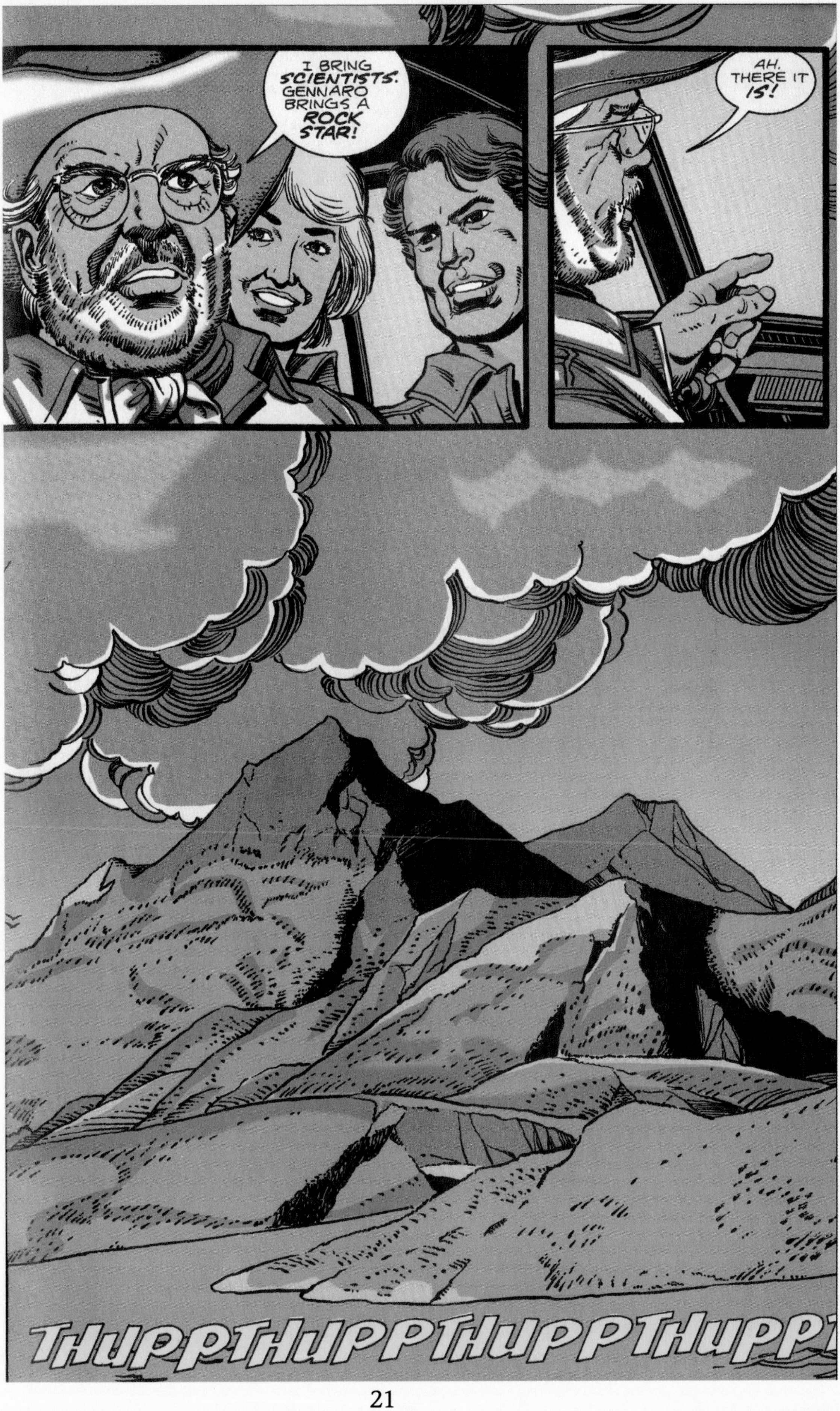
I BRING SCIENTISTS. GENNARO BRINGS A ROCK STAR!
AH. THERE IT IS!
THUPPTHUPPTHUPPTHUPP

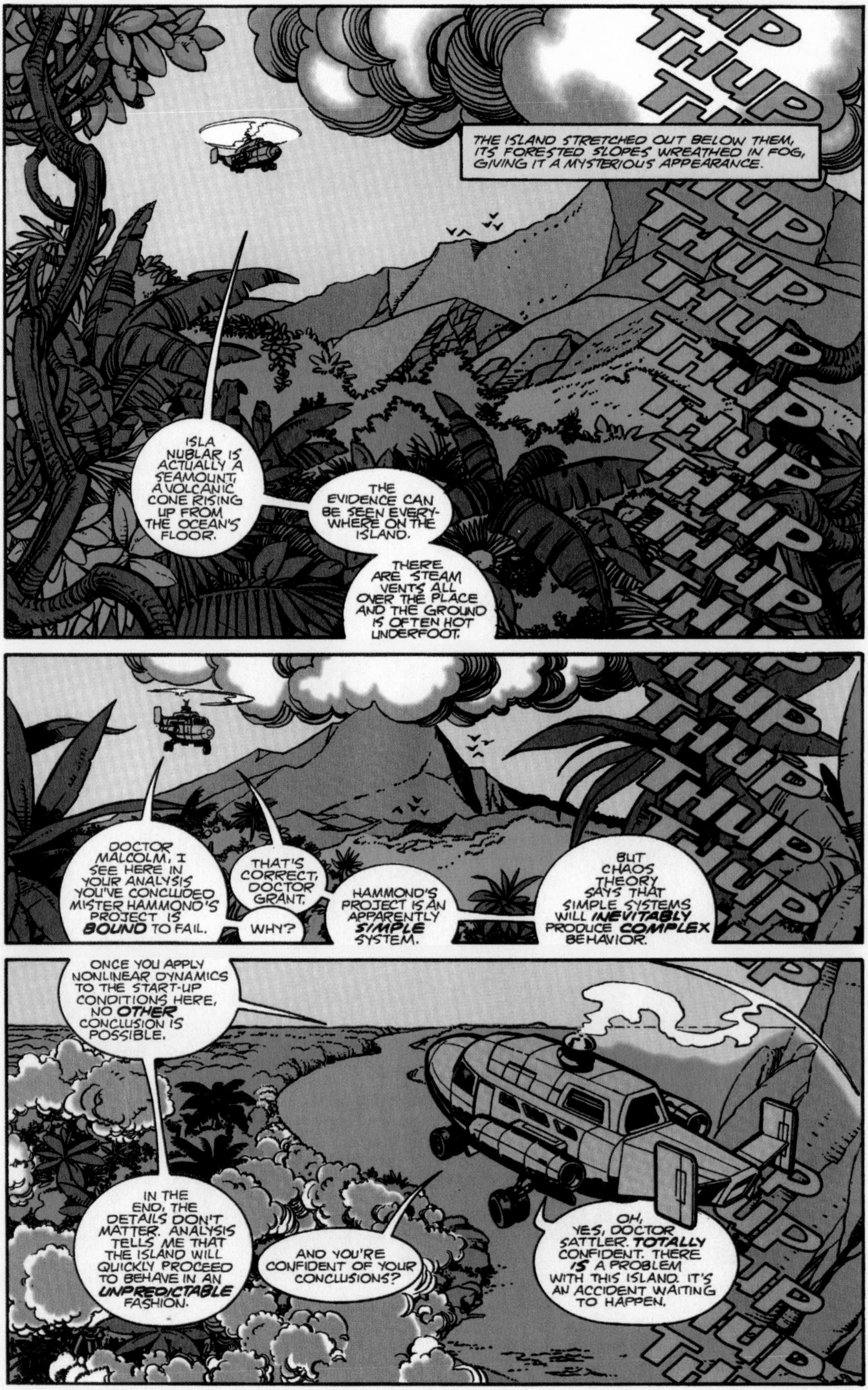
THUP
THE ISLAND STRETCHED OUT BELOW THEM, ITS FORESTED SLOPES WREATHED IN FOG, GIVING IT A MYSTERIOUS APPEARANCE.
THUP THUP THUP THUP THUP THUP THUP THUP THUP
ISLA NUBLAR IS ACTUALLY A SEAMOUNT, A VOLCANIC CONE RISING UP FROM THE OCEAN'S FLOOR.
THE EVIDENCE CAN BE SEEN EVERYWHERE ON THE ISLAND.
THERE ARE STEAM VENTS ALL OVER THE PLACE AND THE GROUND IS OFTEN HOT UNDERFOOT.
THUP THUP THUP THUP
DOCTOR MALCOLM, I SEE HERE IN YOUR ANALYSIS YOU'VE CONCLUDED MISTER HAMMOND'S PROJECT IS BOUND TO FAIL.
THAT'S CORRECT, DOCTOR GRANT.
WHY?
HAMMOND'S PROJECT IS AN APPARENTLY SIMPLE SYSTEM.
BUT CHAOS THEORY SAYS THAT SIMPLE SYSTEMS WILL INEVITABLY PRODUCE COMPLEX BEHAVIOR.
ONCE YOU APPLY NONLINEAR DYNAMICS TO THE START-UP CONDITIONS HERE, NO OTHER CONCLUSION IS POSSIBLE.
IN THE END, THE DETAILS DON'T MATTER. ANALYSIS TELLS ME THAT THE ISLAND WILL QUICKLY PROCEED TO BEHAVE IN AN UNPREDICTABLE FASHION.
AND YOU'RE CONFIDENT OF YOUR CONCLUSIONS?
OH, YES, DOCTOR SATTLER. TOTALLY CONFIDENT. THERE IS A PROBLEM WITH THIS ISLAND. IT'S AN ACCIDENT WAITING TO HAPPEN.
THUP THUP THUP

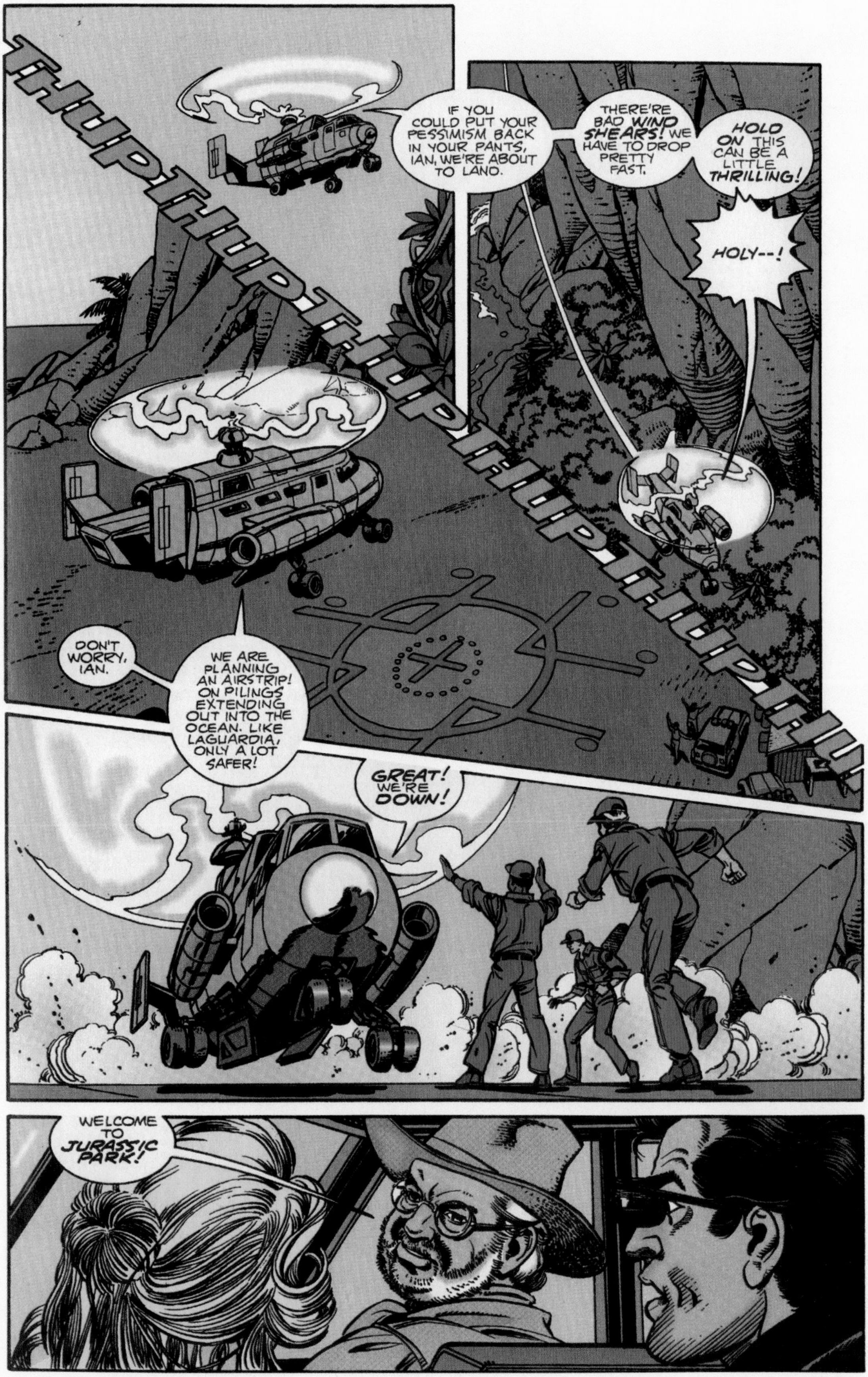

THUP THUP THUP THUP THUP THUP THUP THU
IF YOU COULD PUT YOUR PESSIMISM BACK IN YOUR PANTS, IAN, WE'RE ABOUT TO LAND.
THERE'RE BAD WIND SHEARS! WE HAVE TO DROP PRETTY FAST.
HOLD ON THIS CAN BE A LITTLE THRILLING!
HOLY--!
DON'T WORRY, IAN.
WE ARE PLANNING AN AIRSTRIP! ON PILINGS EXTENDING OUT INTO THE OCEAN. LIKE LAGUARDIA, ONLY A LOT SAFER!
GREAT! WE'RE DOWN!
WELCOME TO JURASSIC PARK!

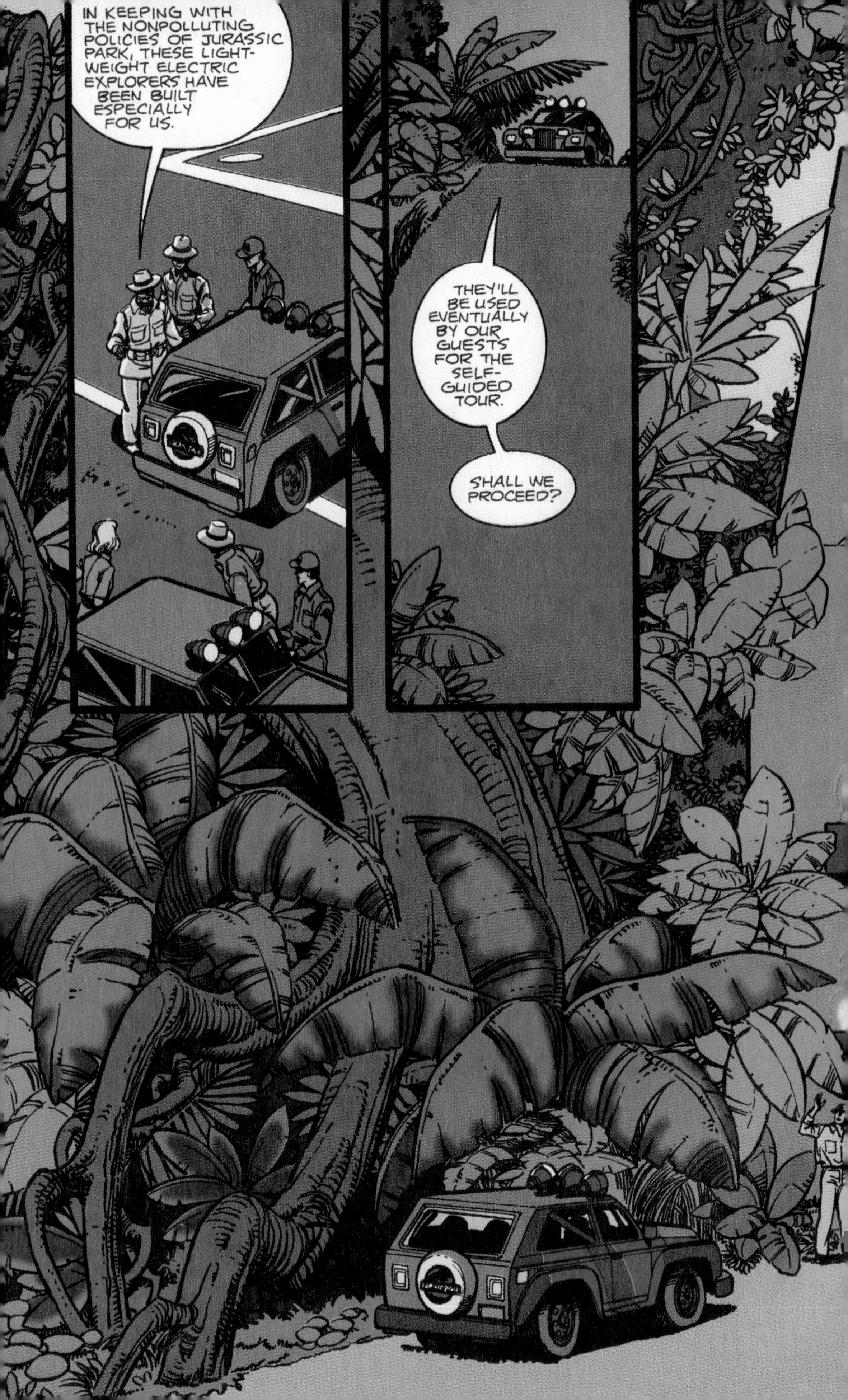
IN KEEPING WITH THE NONPOLLUTING POLICIES OF JURASSIC PARK, THESE LIGHT-WEIGHT ELECTRIC EXPLORERS HAVE BEEN BUILT ESPECIALLY FOR US.
THEY'LL BE USED EVENTUALLY BY OUR GUESTS FOR THE SELF-GUIDED TOUR.
SHALL WE PROCEED?

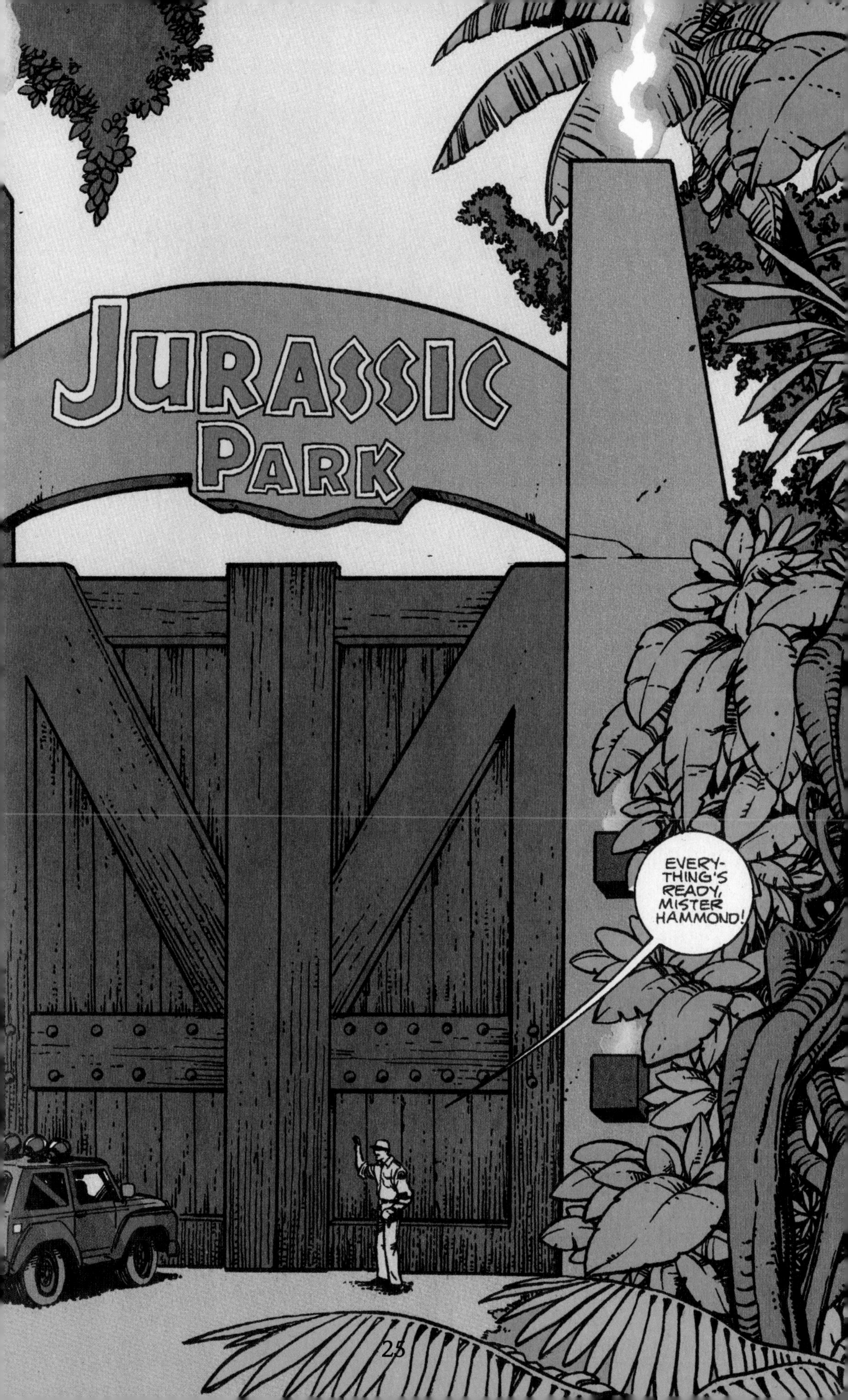
JURASSIC PARK
EVERY-THING'S READY, MISTER HAMMOND!

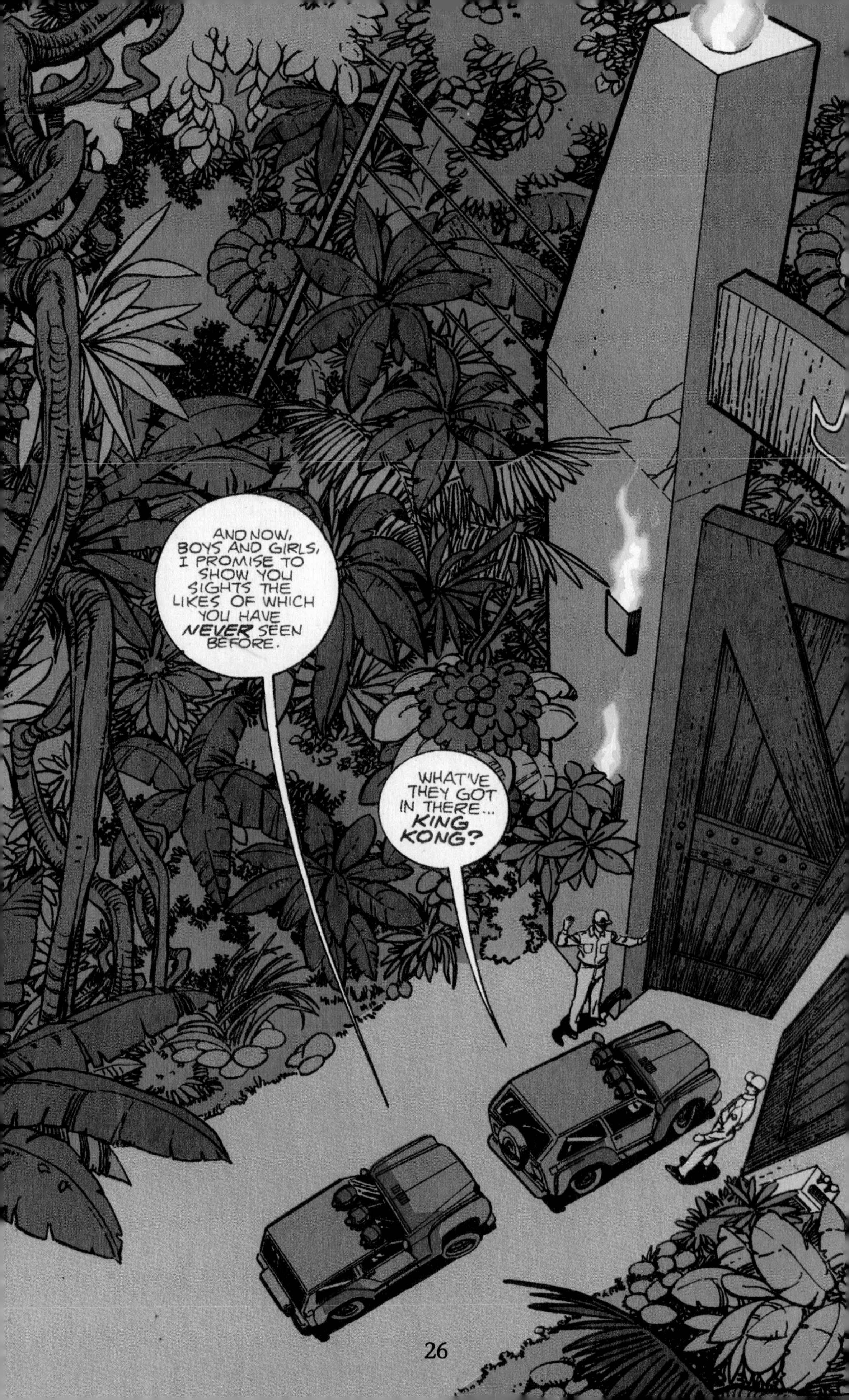
AND NOW, BOYS AND GIRLS, I PROMISE TO SHOW YOU SIGHTS THE LIKES OF WHICH YOU HAVE NEVER SEEN BEFORE.
WHAT'VE THEY GOT IN THERE... KING KONG?

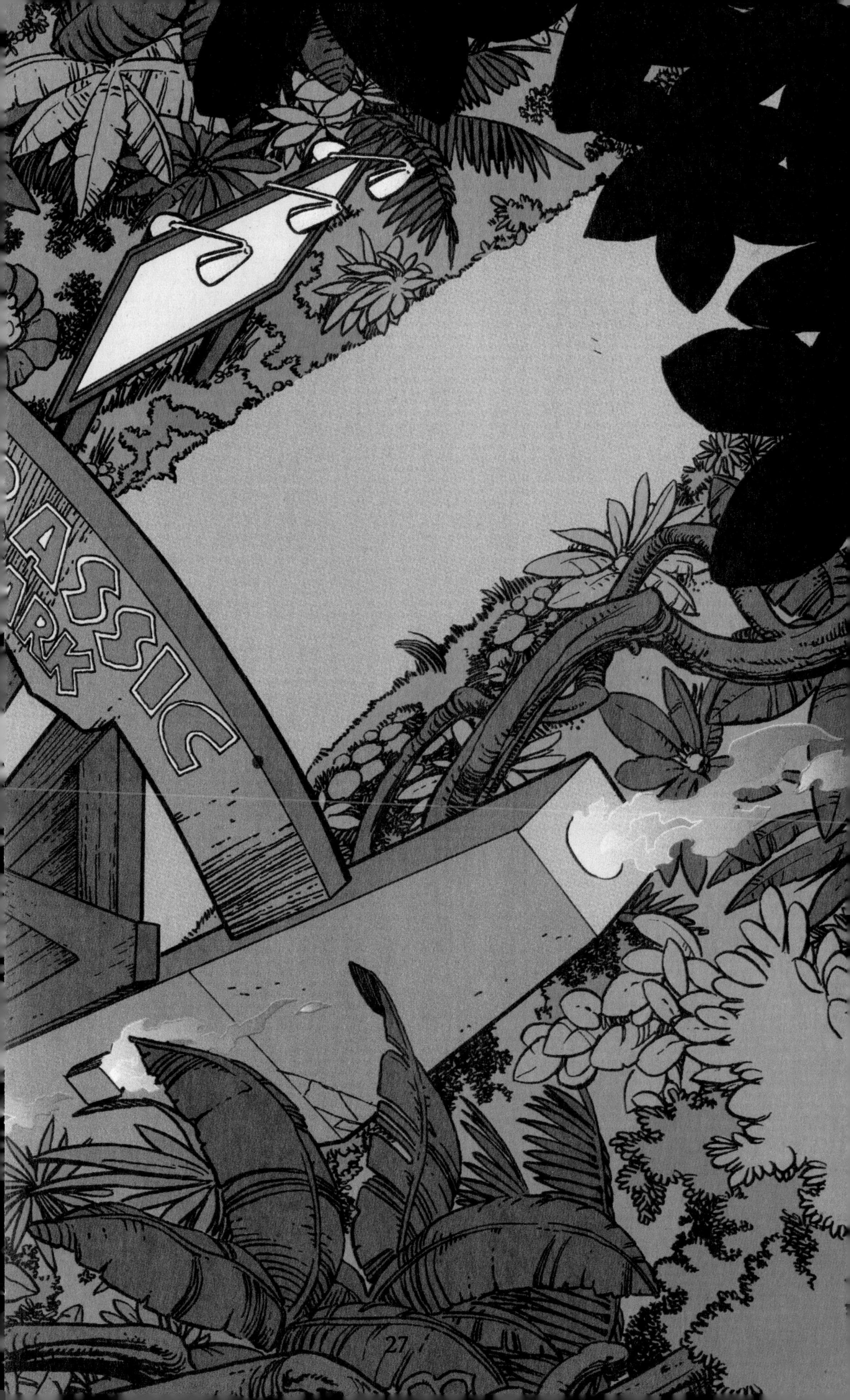
ASSIC
ARK

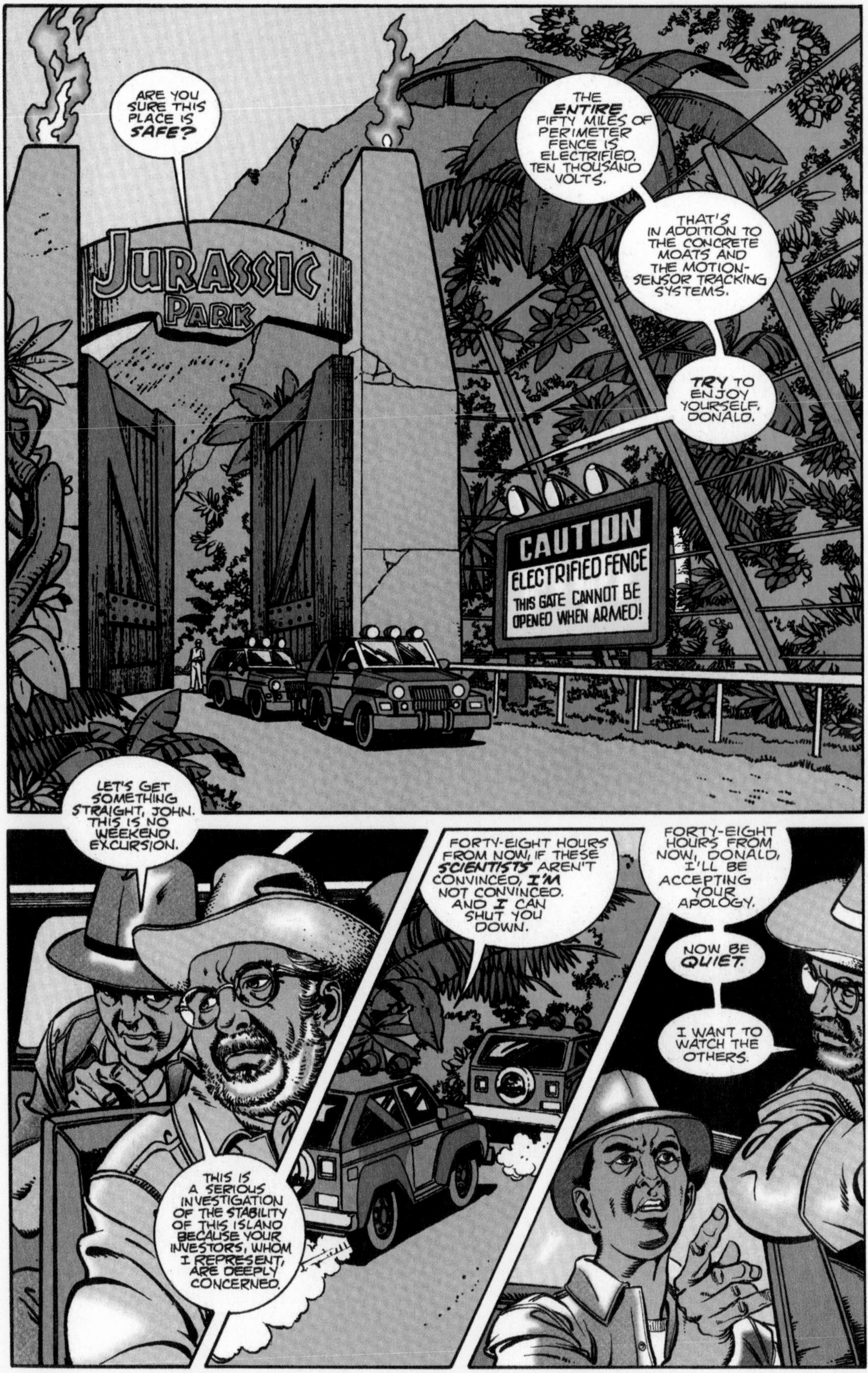
ARE YOU SURE THIS PLACE IS SAFE?
JURASSIC PARK
THE ENTIRE FIFTY MILES OF PERIMETER FENCE IS ELECTRIFIED. TEN THOUSAND VOLTS.
THAT'S IN ADDITION TO THE CONCRETE MOATS AND THE MOTION-SENSOR TRACKING SYSTEMS.
TRY TO ENJOY YOURSELF, DONALD.
CAUTION
ELECTRIFIED FENCE
THIS GATE CANNOT BE OPENED WHEN ARMED!
LET'S GET SOMETHING STRAIGHT, JOHN. THIS IS NO WEEKEND EXCURSION.
THIS IS A SERIOUS INVESTIGATION OF THE STABILITY OF THIS ISLAND BECAUSE YOUR INVESTORS, WHOM I REPRESENT, ARE DEEPLY CONCERNED.
FORTY-EIGHT HOURS FROM NOW, IF THESE SCIENTISTS AREN'T CONVINCED, I'M NOT CONVINCED. AND I CAN SHUT YOU DOWN.
FORTY-EIGHT HOURS FROM NOW, DONALD, I'LL BE ACCEPTING YOUR APOLOGY.
NOW BE QUIET.
I WANT TO WATCH THE OTHERS.

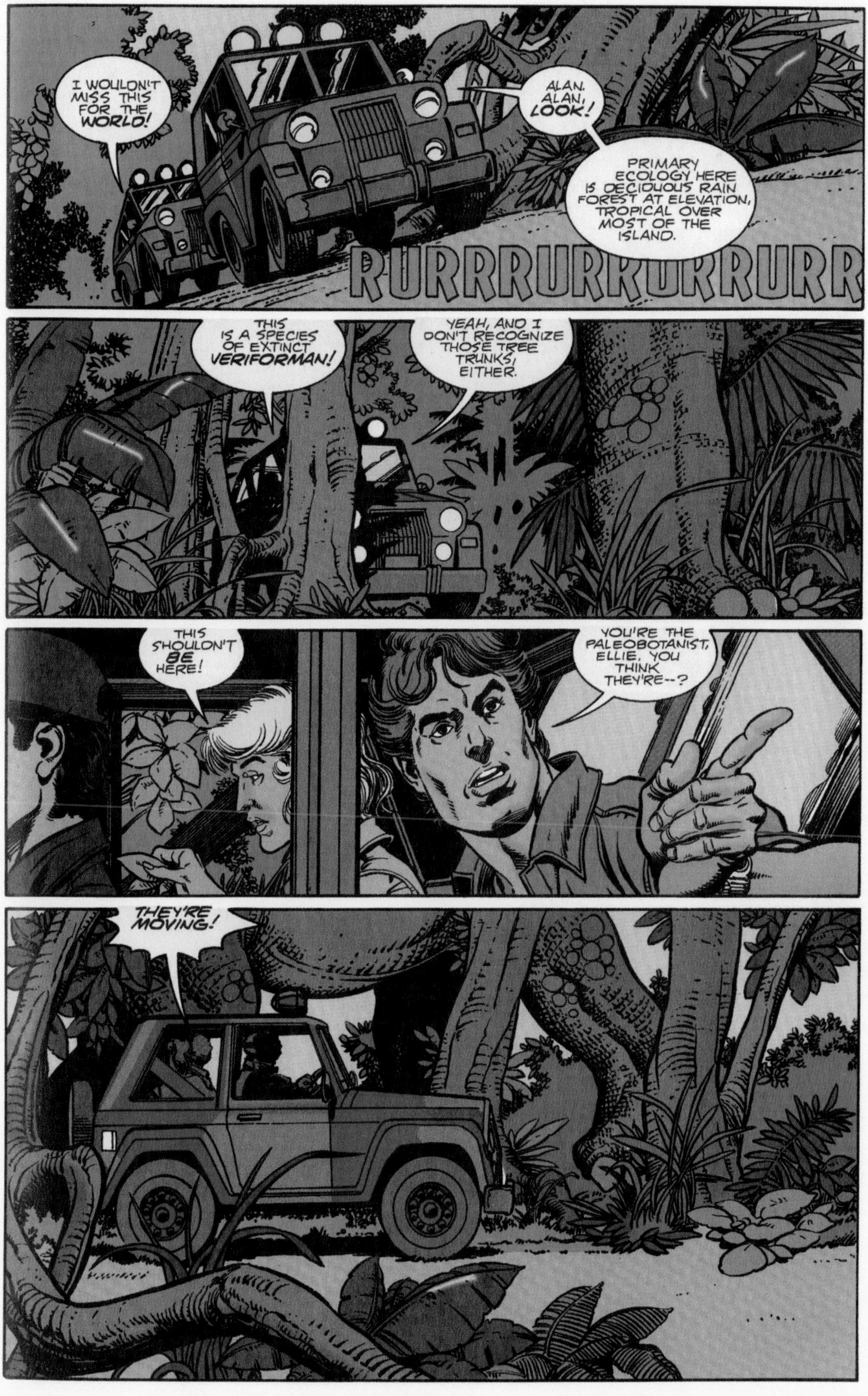
I WOULDN'T MISS THIS FOR THE WORLD!
ALAN. ALAN, LOOK!
PRIMARY ECOLOGY HERE IS DECIDUOUS RAIN FOREST AT ELEVATION, TROPICAL OVER MOST OF THE ISLAND.
RURRRURRURRURR
THIS IS A SPECIES OF EXTINCT VERIFORMAN!
YEAH, AND I DON'T RECOGNIZE THOSE TREE TRUNKS, EITHER.
THIS SHOULDN'T BE HERE!
YOU'RE THE PALEOBOTANIST, ELLIE. YOU THINK THEY'RE--?
THEY'RE MOVING!

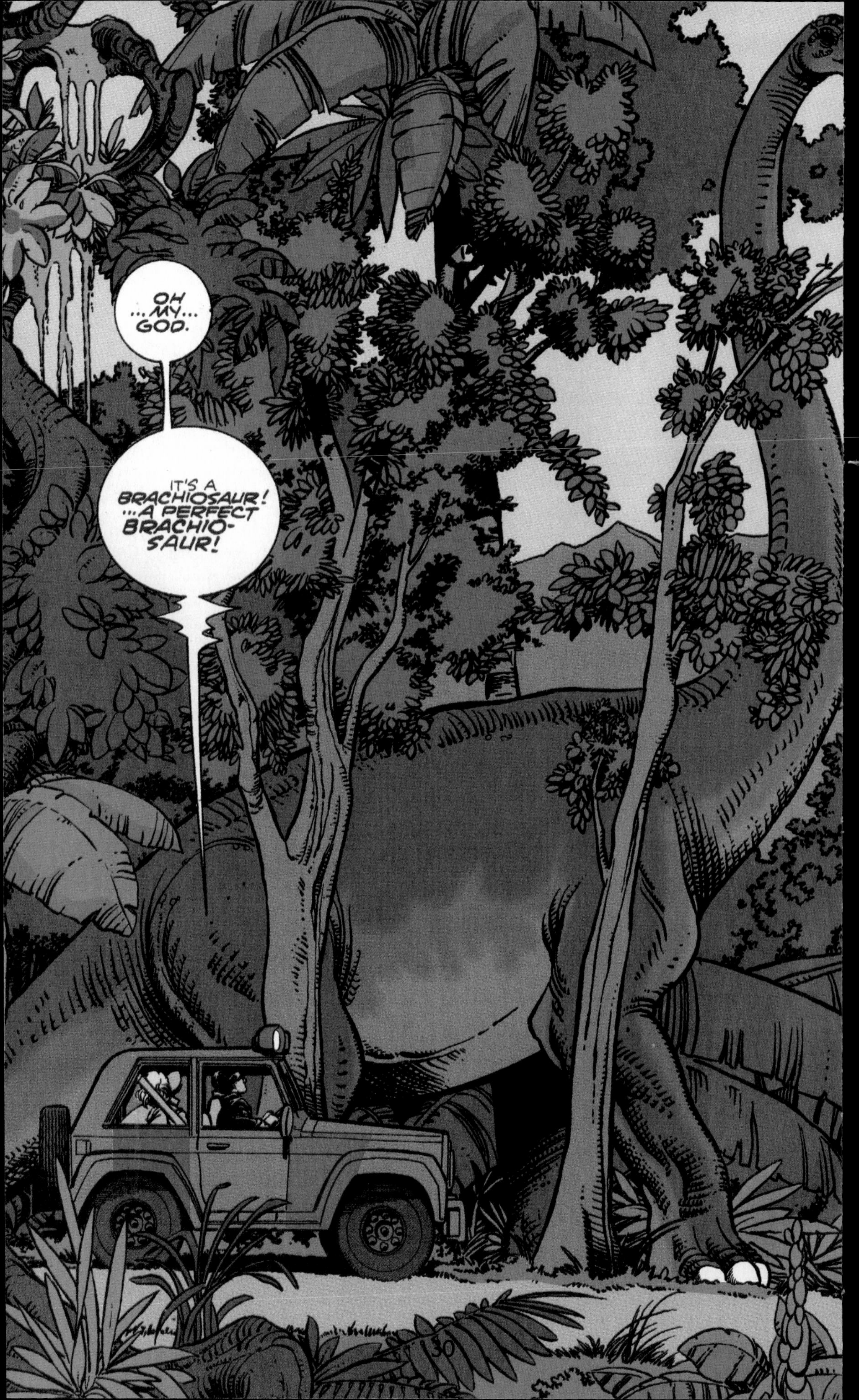
OH ...MY... GOD.
IT'S A BRACHIOSAUR! ...A PERFECT BRACHIO-SAUR!

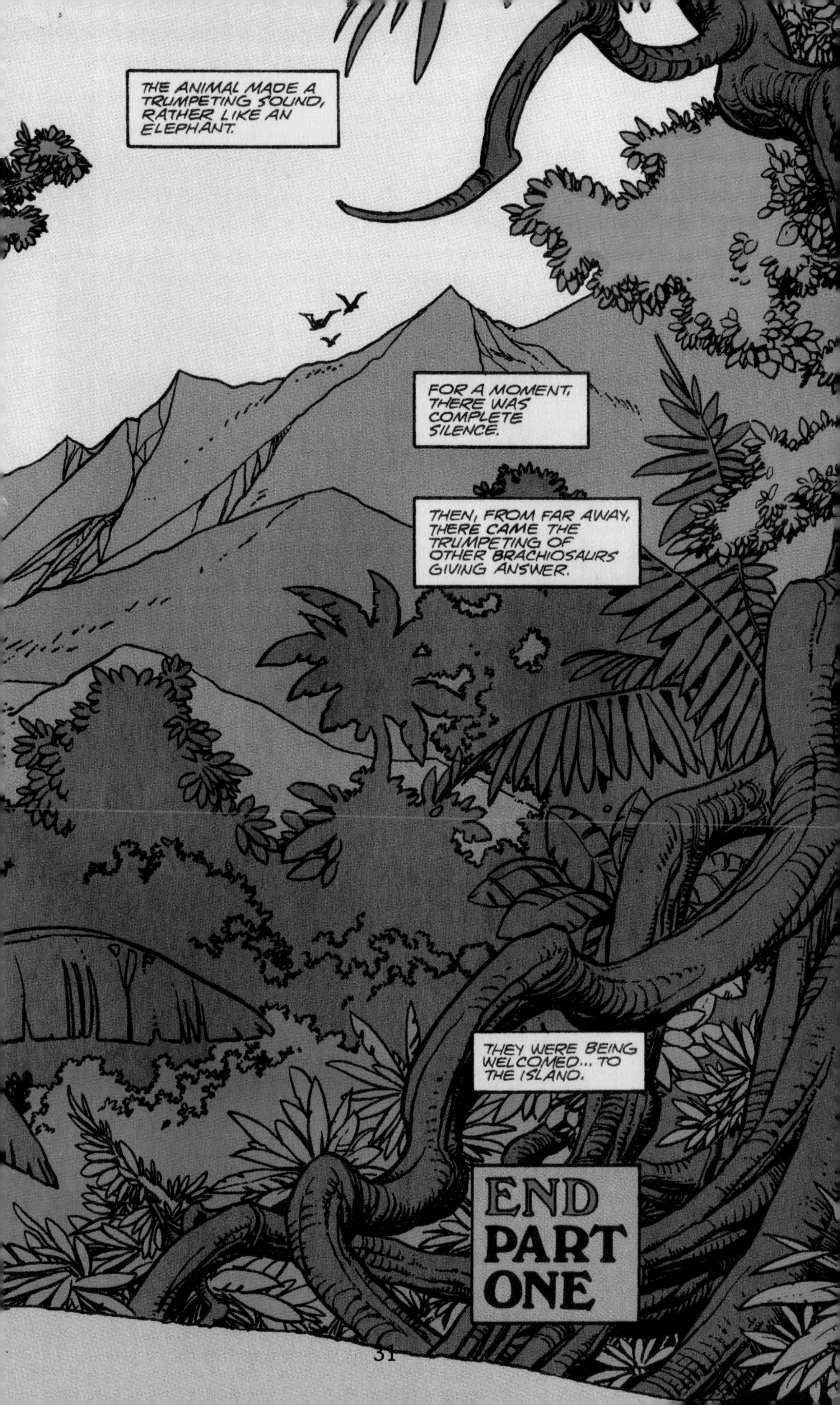
THE ANIMAL MADE A TRUMPETING SOUND, RATHER LIKE AN ELEPHANT.
FOR A MOMENT, THERE WAS COMPLETE SILENCE.
THEN, FROM FAR AWAY, THERE CAME THE TRUMPETING OF OTHER BRACHIOSAURS GIVING ANSWER.
THEY WERE BEING WELCOMED... TO THE ISLAND.
END PART ONE